CONFESSIONS
OF
A HIGH LAMA

The Path of Return

Omnilux®

SAMAHRIA RAMSEN

Author of Kiss of Karma
A Tale of a Yogi
Who Fell in Love With a Courtesan

Published by Omnilux Communications Inc.
P.O Box 58101, 3089 Dufferin St. Toronto, ON, Canada, M6A 3C8

Omnilux Publisher's Books and Posters may be purchased for inspirational, educational, business, or sales promotional use. For information please visit:
www.omniluxcommunications.com

Library of Congress Cataloguing-in-Publication Data
Ramsen, Samahria
Confessions of a high lama: the path of return / Samahria Ramsen
ISBN 978-0-9699078-6-2
1.Title
PS8635.A465C66 2007
C2007-903809-3   C813'.6

Fiction / Inspirational Romantic Fantasy

To My Teacher

CONTENTS

Author's Note

PART ONE - THE URGE FOR CONFESSION

PART TWO – CONFESSION

"When all desires that surge in the heart
Are renounced, the mortal becomes
immortal.
When all the knots that strangle the heart
Are loosened, the mortal becomes
immortal.
This sums up the teachings of the
scriptures."

Katha Upanishad
2:14-15

Author's Note

"Confessions of a High Lama" is a journey of love. We often take this journey without recognizing it; for most of us are caught up in the web of our daily mundane challenges of existence.

I wrote this book to awaken the dormant volcano of yearning to love that is aching to explode in most of us.

The path from the womb to the tomb is what we call life; and it must be exciting. Otherwise we have lived in vain.

In today's world of audited love, starting with a dating service and planning a family, as we would plan our business or our jobs, we have truly lost the rapture of life. Instead, many of us have left the expectation of this rapture for a later time; and that is beyond the tomb.

I composed the "Confessions of a High Lama" to open the heart and to take a peek at our soul and acknowledge our soul mate in our imagination.

To fall in love is a heroic act. We transform our individuality and become a new person in union with our soul mate. We cease to exist and experience paradise right here in our mind.

There is a hero in each one of us. A hero gives up himself for a higher purpose, embraces it, and becomes transformed. You will experience your own heroic heart in your own individualized journey with the High Lama.

I trust that "Confessions..." will open up your mind and let the ecstasy pour out from your soul; and lead you to a serene spot, where you will cherish love and turmoil, lust and anguish; and where desire will blossom in your heart.

Samahria Ramsen

PART ONE

THE URGE
FOR
CONFESSION

CHAPTER 1

THE

ENCHANTRESS

Living in Parallel

Universes at the Same Time

The flame in the hurricane lantern was flickering in the darkness of the little hut. Yet it seemed luminous from the light, radiating from the old mystic. The flickering of the flame of the lantern was shyly dancing on the face of this Master in total humility and in adoration of life, as the enchanting woman was sitting in front of this magnificent man. She had come to the Master to seek answers of the past to understand her turbulent present.

Outside, where the hut sat snugly, was the physical dwelling place of this realized Consciousness of the Master of Ram Shankar Roy.

The music of the night was humming the charming tune of the Himalayan grove. The stillness of the dark valley was singing the hymn of praise to the beauty of this enchantress.

"You seek answers of life and not of Ram," resounded the Master in a deep whisper.

Natasha looked at him with awe and reverence and replied in urgent quest and certainty:

"I know that my Ram lives and I know that you have the answers. I am prepared to travel the path through time and space to reunite with my love, as I have done a thousand times before. Only this time I want it to be the last. I want to merge with my Ram and end this illusion of pain and pleasure. Please help me to find him, Master."

The old mystic closed his eyes and in a flash saw the endless chain of events that created this moment and brought this enchanting woman to the small Himalayan village.

He saw Natasha, as a beautiful courtesan named Urvashi in her last incarnation, living in the Golden Age of India, deeply entangled in the games of life, filled with decadent pleasures and dreadful pains. There was nothing left for her that could attract or give her joy, as if she had exhausted the endless cycle of life and death.

He saw the intense urge of this gorgeous enchantress, aching to find the secret of eternal youth. He saw the many ways which she had travelled to realize her dream, until she met the sage Agustya, a mystic, who knew the secret of life.

He saw Agustya with the eyes of that heavenly enchantress, an irresistible god-man in his divine wholeness, combining all the moods and emotions that she had experienced in her entire life.

He witnessed a moment of eternal forgetfulness, a forbidden love of a heavenly courtesan and a sage, which culminated into the birth of Sangita, their daughter, who never knew her mother and her father.

The old Master opened his eyes and saw the same beautiful courtesan, sitting in front of him in total surrender; but now she was named Natasha Roy and was dressed in 21st Century clothes, fully ready to climb the mountains or ride on the back of a horse in order to find her beloved sage.

The Master knew everything about her. He saw her past, present, and future when he had performed the wedding ceremony of Natasha and Ram eight months ago, right here in this village.

"The unfinished kiss had urged your soul to come back," said the Master with the affection of a father. "That is why you are here now, my daughter."

Natasha lowered her eyes, smiled inwardly, and asked in a trembling voice:

"Can you tell me more, Master?"

"Destiny, my daughter, has brought you to this very moment of knowing the truth of existence; of knowing your purpose, and of completing the passion of that unfinished kiss."

The Master touched Natasha's forehead between her eyebrows with his right thumb; and she lost consciousness of this Universe and awoke in another parallel Universe knowing that she had belonged here before.

The Master took her on a journey to retrace her life from the past. She saw herself being groomed as a courtesan. She saw kings swoon at her feet to taste the nectar of her beauty. She felt the agony of the embrace of passion with no love. She danced, but could not feel the thunder of the heavens in her heart. She felt an emptiness that could not be filled with all the passion of the Universe, till she met the great sage Agustya in the forest beside the giggling brook and fell in love with him.

"The agony of love of a mortal is unknown to a mortal. To taste the bliss of love you must become a goddess."

Natasha heard the voice, but did not know where this voice was coming from. She thought that it was the voice of Ram, but was not sure. The same voice resounded again, breaking the silence of the void:

"I made you into a goddess, and then I loved you. Don't become human. Humans cannot love…"

Natasha did not know where she was. It seemed that she was living in two Universes at the same time, whirling in an endless dance of seduction; enchanting and conquering, until she was finally conquered.

A trained lover and the most beautiful courtesan of the Golden Age of India, who made love her profession, found herself in love with no path of return.

Was it Agustya or Ram? She did not know. Time
and space vanished. She was effortlessly traveling from
the forest of the enlightened civilization of the 5th Century
B.C. to the tumultuous concrete jungle of 21st Century
modern world. She was everywhere and everywhen at the
same time.

Natasha found herself transported into the pleasure
palace of a mighty emperor. This was a hall of pleasure,
not of love; a hall of lust, not of laughter. She was waiting
to dance for the most powerful man of the times. The hall
was lit by a thousand candles. The jeweled chandeliers
reflected a million rays of light; and the dance of the
flames was almost provoking her to start dancing to the
rhythm of the challenging laughter of the thousand flames.

She stood still in the center of the mosaic floor
that was invoking her to dance. She felt that it was a
moment of destiny, a looming crucial encounter that was
going to put her life into a whirlpool of love, lust, and
intrigue. She was waiting for the Emperor.

The Emperor loved her the moment he laid his
eyes on her from a distance. He knew who she was. He
had seen her before in the mount of Sarnath where the
great Gotama gave his sermon. It was the place of
pilgrimage for her.

On every full moon night she danced for love and
her audiences were the spirits of the Masters and the Great
Gotama.

21

She danced; her body moved. The companionless moon blushed with envy at her beauty, trying to reflect more of the light of the Sun.

She danced to invoke her love for Agustya, the man and the sage. She yearned for his embrace and for becoming one with him. She knew he would come; but it was the Emperor Samudragupta that saw her that night and fell in love with her.

Now she stood on the floor of this magnificent pleasure palace, waiting to bestow pleasure to a man.

She knew men. She knew that beneath the crowns and all the titles a man was a slave to beauty that oozes lust. She could flood the whole palace with her lust.

The Emperor walked in the hall. He was all alone with no entourage or body guards. He was in love.

She did not love him. She couldn't. She had given her soul to Agustya. She knew that she could saturate the Emperor with pleasure and the Emperor would become oblivious to this magnificent pleasure palace and his empire, but she could not give him her love.

She heard the voice of the Master. He said:

"My daughter, the Emperor Samudragupta could not get your love as a woman; that is why he has now come to get your love as a daughter."

In a flash she saw the same Emperor as a different man with a different look, wearing different clothes. She saw him picking her up from her bed, when she was a child.

Then she was transported into a Himalayan mountain region, filled with aromas of spicy bushes. Now she was a young woman, walking through the rose garden with the same man. He looked different again. Yet, she felt that she knew who he was. She wanted to call him father and give him an embrace, as she did when she was a child.

"Papa, is it proper for me to call you papa here?" she asked. "Is it proper for you to give me an embrace?"

He looked at her and said: "It is more than proper. Even in the next kingdom, even in the next world."

She felt the warmth of his breath, followed by a gentle kiss on her forehead. His strong arms circled around her slender body, protecting her from all seeming troubles of the world. She surrendered in his arms. Time stopped. Nothing existed outside this divine, perfect moment of union.

"You made peace with your past, my daughter," said the Master. "Now you shall finish the unfinished kiss."

CHAPTER 2

BEHIND
THE
MASK

The Man

Who Was Loved and Feared

A turbulent dialogue between his mind and his heart ceased. The High Lama saw himself as he was: without pretences, without an armor of power, and without the mask of a stoic man fighting for his ideals of greatness and well-being of others.

Slowly he was able to remove the invisible divide he developed, which was protecting him from himself, and to face his own soul.

Now, face to face with his problem, he had to admit that he had failed his daughter again. He was not able to convince Natasha that Ram was not what she imagined. That he was not just a professor of transformational psychology, but also a cold blooded assassin that would not hesitate to kill for his ideals.

"Where are you now, my daughter?" He whispered, looking through the open window of his office into a pitch dark night.

"Forgive me that I couldn't protect you. Perhaps you are blinded by love and cannot see. I was in your shoes once. And I had lost your mother. I want to help you. I want to free you from Ram."

The High Lama suddenly felt pangs in his heart. The unknown emotions brought tears to his eyes. Covered by darkness, he silently wept, releasing a torturous throbbing pain from his heart.

For a moment he felt a sense of freedom, a sense of relief from a lifetime of entrapment created by his own ego. He realized that he took birth not for this entrapment, but for something much greater. He saw that all of his life was simply a game, an exploration, and an adventure.

Yet he was amazed at how quickly he lost himself in the ego driven senses, in that illusionary greatness which he had created for himself. And how quickly he allowed himself to get entrapped by his own game, become immersed into the affairs of the world; and finally get caught into his own web to learn about his pains, his fears, and his death.

He allowed himself to become a man, forgetting that he was God, the divine essence of life, the divine intelligence that brought him here to create these very experiences and illusions.

The cold north-west wind rushed through the open window of his room, cooling his head and drying unwanted tears. He did not know what had happened to him. Time stopped while he was silently turning the pages of his life, filled with risks and adventures.

Was it a moment, or was it two thousand years that passed? Who knows? The game was enchanting... Everything seemed to have had a purpose and reason...

Slowly the High Lama began to believe that the game he played was his only reality; and that he must stay on guard to protect himself from the dark forces of the opposition.

With time he developed the attitude of survival that diminished the flow of the life-force inherent in him, and his body began to age. Yet, he was pushing on...

Depriving himself of the simple joys of ordinary people, the High Lama began to build the illusory walls of protection around him. His ego made him forget his divine essence, and his real purpose.

Fooling himself by this self-inflicted greatness, he developed his own truth and began to interpret it according to his own corrupted beliefs.

With time his well hidden fears began to take over his consciousness. His power of reason lost its sharpness and brought frequent thoughts of death.

Being a powerful man, he was able to control his melancholic thoughts knowing that it does not take long for a thought to become a pattern and bring with it a cellular change of his body. Knowing all that, he did not allow himself this weakness.

The High Lama was not only an influential, powerful, and controlling man, but also attractive. He had a beautiful demeanor that demanded obedience and reverence at the same time. He had a smile and a confidence about him that was so captivating, charming, and magnetic that people would offer no resistance and do anything to get his approval.

He was loved and he was feared at the same time. Yet inside he was a terrified man, terrified of himself, and not of anyone else. He did not even like his own reflection in the mirror. He always had to have other things reflected with him. Every time, when there was nothing else in the mirror but him, he was seeing a river, flowing with blood. He was seeing a mass destruction of lives. And he was the organizer and director of all these, which had to be supposedly done for peace, harmony, and joy.

His whole life was a contradiction; and he could not resolve this paradox, for there was no resolution.

Perhaps one day, he thought, he will be able to resolve with Natasha, but with Ram? Can he ever resolve with Ram? He loved Ram, but he could never trust him, as he could never trust himself.

The High Lama could not believe that Ram could change; and he had all the reasons for that. He himself was the reason.

A complicated man, the High Lama was desperately trying to find a solution to his problem. Like the scorpion from the ancient fable, he was looking for an opportunity to befriend the frog and make the frog take him across the river. But the scorpion and the frog cannot be friends.

The north-west wind gathered its force. Heavy clouds pregnant with the water of life were rushing towards the sleepy valley.

The High Lama was still awake in the middle of the night. Sitting motionless in his deep comfortable chair, he was more turbulent inside than the stormy night was outside.

The north-west wind smashed at his window, entered his room, and touched the High Lama's face with a wet moist kiss. The exquisite aromas of the rose garden filled up his room, but the High Lama couldn't feel the delight of the night. His heart was restless, heavy with pain, and full of suppressed longings.

He had developed a practice of sitting in his comfortable chair for some time before falling asleep. Tonight sleep was reluctant to come. He hesitated... Then, for the first time in his life, he allowed himself to think the thoughts he wanted to think.

He was hesitant to face the truth; afraid that his own feelings could be more important than all the great ideals to which he had dedicated his entire life.

The yearning to love engulfed him. He felt the sensation of joy that was forbidden to enter his life. A warm smile animated his face, but he still questioned himself. He could not believe that this could be what his heart was aching for.

And immediately the High Lama's intellect took over his heart and reminded him that he was not an ordinary man; that he was not allowed to think of his own joys when the whole world was in turmoil and pain; and that he was not born for his own pleasures, but for justice and balance in the world.

The old pains and longings surfaced again. Darkness penetrated the High Lama's heart. He did not understand what was bothering him. He felt a sensation, a sense of deja-vu. He was getting flashes of illusions, which made him feel what he was feeling.

He was trying to find the reason behind these feelings, and influence himself by his own greatness.

"Nobody knows me," he thought. "And nobody can even understand me. I am invincible, yet I feel so vulnerable. I can destroy Ram. Yet, something stops me from doing it.

My daughter left. She doesn't love me. She thinks about me as a monstrosity. She does not understand my tenderness, and rejects my love. And I also don't understand her. How can I see and feel what she sees and feels? This is the weakness that I have never experienced before in this external world."

This man, the High Lama, who can make and break worlds for people, suddenly was confronted with his own world, his own life, and everything became so meaningless without the resolution of this situation.

"I want love," he screamed silently. "Give me some love, my daughter. Enter my heart and enter my duties, and then you might feel what I am feeling."

The High Lama did not know that he had experienced the same feelings before, two thousand years ago. He did not know that he was the king Samudragupta, who fell in love with Urvashi, the most beautiful courtesan living on earth at that time. Urvashi loved another man, the sage from the forest. And the king killed the man she loved to have her all to himself.

But there is Karma, the law of cause and effect. And nothing will ever escape this law. And no karmic debts will be left unpaid.

At that moment the High Lama did not know that the main reason for his reincarnation was not to change the world, but to change himself. That was why he felt tormented. That was why he hesitated to commit a similar murder in a similar situation.

Each one of us is re-born for the same reason: to change ourselves, to fulfill unfulfilled desires, to advance and progress. Yet, each one of us designs our own tests and trials.

There is always a choice to be made, and the choice is ours. Some might choose to go back rather than forward; and that is extremely painful, a tormenting, and degrading experience, a torture for the soul.

Now, once again, the High Lama was about to design his own destiny, the destination of his own choosing. He felt that he was standing on the precipice of defeat; one wrong step and he could fall and be destroyed. Yet he would rather die than be defeated.

"My daughter," he cried, "Don't make me into a victim. I have never been conquered, and I will never accept defeat. I am torn apart, look into my heart. I love Ram and I love you, Natasha. Yet, I have my duties to fulfill.

"Ram, my comrade, my son, my best trained man, tell me, what shall I do with you?"

He was asking himself the same questions a thousand times. He knew that by setting the trap and destroying Ram, he would also destroy his daughter's life. And he was sure that Natasha would never forgive him for doing that.

His knees wobbled. He suddenly had a vision that lasted only a moment but felt like a lifetime. He saw the face of a woman with a smile equally attractive and terrifying. He felt that it was the smile of death itself, careless of all that he was afraid to lose. Deep in his thoughts he said:

"Don't leave me Urvashi. I love you, and I love my brother Agustya. Yet, I have my duties to fulfill. I am torn apart between my duties and my feelings."

The mysterious face of a woman had vanished. Yet the High Lama's heart continued to tremble and long for something that he could not explain; something that he knew, but could not remember.

He listened for a while to his own heart beat, as if it could tell him the way out from this uneasy situation created by his own past deeds.

Suddenly he heard a soft quiet voice whispering in his ear:

"Wait! You have all the power to kill Ram, yet in Ram's death is hidden your own death."

It was the voice of Ram's Master. He was certain. He knew that if Ram was alive, the only way he could find him was through Ram's Master. He also had a compelling desire to find the Master and make him his confessor.

CHAPTER 3

THE

URGE

FOR CONFESSION

The Yearning for Release

From Self Deprivation

The pressing urge to confess was as unbalanced as the High Lama's life had been. He had killed to love and had become an invisible despot. He wanted to destroy Ram with a clean heart or at least justify to himself his action. His instinct of using people led him to the extent of having the intention of exploiting a Master, a Godman.

It was not to be so. The High Lama didn't know that this corrupting urge would lead to his salvation. He did not waste a single moment. This impulse drove him to take the journey through the same terrain that Natasha took to unite in marriage with Ram. The path was known to him and the same young Sherpa took him to the doorstep of the Master.

The Master was not there. Was it by design or was it by coincidence? The Master was in another village for a spiritual gathering. The High Lama did not have any choice but to wait for the Master to come back.

The vibration of the hut was an enchanting cosmic symphony. While waiting, the High Lama lost track of time and space. He felt that he was transported into the region of his soul that he had never seen before.

He was exploring... He became the mirror of his own consciousness. He was being prepared to meet the Master by the Master. The High Lama's salvation from the bondage of a lifeless life was at hand.

In that moment of eternity he was shown his own ideology and saw the paradox of his purpose. He recognized the aphorism: "The road to hell is paved with good intentions".

He wanted peace and tranquility in everybody's life. And yet, he was using disharmony and aggression to bring that about. He was justifying killing to bring peace. He was justifying deception to bring love and tranquility into individual lives. And he felt that he was doing the same with his own daughter.

The High Lama was a complicated man. Yet there was a lot of love in his heart unexpressed, or rather, suppressed. His own deception deprived him from the greatest romance he ever had, romance with Natasha's mother. Slowly he had suppressed and then buried his feelings, justifying his actions by his worldly ideals.

For a moment he entered his stillness, and in that stillness there were memories, reflections, and order. He crossed the threshold of his desire centre. And there he saw the beauty and the laughter of the woman who gave birth to his daughter.

He never realized how gentle and how tender that woman was. He saw the sparkle in her eyes when she pressed Natasha for the first time against her breasts.

"What did I sacrifice that eternity for?" He asked himself. "Was it for an ideal that was implanted in my heart for the betterment of this world? What is the world? Is the world my responsibility? No! I failed my life and my responsibility. I want to go back," the High Lama said aloud.

Yet he knew that there was no going back. He knew that his ideals, his ideology, destroyed him. He felt like a monkey who was stung by a wasp. A monkey cannot stand still; but stung by a wasp it becomes mad. He was also stung by a wasp, a demon called ideology.

All of a sudden the High Lama realized that he was fading into a very ordinary thought process.

"Why do I allow myself to think this way?" He immediately asked himself, mentally admitting a great confusion.

"Why am I thinking about all these things at this stage of my life? It annihilates all ideology. It annihilates all principles. It annihilates the very power that gives me power. Am I losing my senses?" He asked himself and was compelled to answer:

"Who needs senses anyways? I want to be ordinary if there is romance in it. I've traveled the world. I've experienced what very few people have experienced, the pleasures of life and of death. I want nothing else but to live.

Then, why do I do all these things? Is it to fill the emptiness in my heart? Is it to give life to others without giving life to myself? Who knows?"

He felt puzzled. There were so many questions and no answers that could give him satisfaction or even bring a moment of peace.

The High Lama was still waiting for the Master to come back. He could not explain what power lured him to stay here. What made him forget his duties? What made him sit still on this straw mattress in front of the empty Master's seat? He felt as if he was held captive by some mysterious energy around him and was not able to break free.

He knew that he came here with one goal And pursuing this goal, he continued to wait to make his confession, without realizing that he was already confessing for many hours.

The dark night enveloped majestic mountains. The sleepless wind stopped for a moment to sing its lullaby to the birds on the tree outside the hut. The High

Lama was listening to the mysterious whispers of the night, saturated with longings.

While the High Lama's mind was fighting his heart and pushing away conflicting feelings, he suddenly felt his daughter's presence around him. He saw her beautiful uncompromising eyes, intensely waiting for his answer. He did not have an answer.

His own flesh and blood, the embodiment of his own spirit was standing before him, seeking love from the man that he had trained to be an assassin.

"What shall I do?" went through his head. "Shall I take the risk and trust Ram after I have taught him that there is no such thing as trust? Am I confused?" he asked himself silently.

"No, I am not confused," was his answer. "I know that I cannot trust Ram. He doesn't have a heart, because I took his heart away."

He could not believe that his daughter, the reflection of the woman that he loved the most, was enticed by Ram.

"She rejected me, her own father, and my ideology, which is identical to Ram's ideology.

What made her accept Ram?" He asked himself. "What does Ram have left after I took everything away from him?"

Surprised and provoked, he could not fathom the answer. He did not know, or did not want to know it. Yet, one thing he knew for sure: he wanted love.

His pounding heart expanded and let a gashing current of love flow out and numb his senses. He felt drowsy, as if he were about to fall asleep.

He was not the High Lama anymore. He was a father, looking at his daughter with his blue eyes, now affectionate and deep, deeper than any ocean, then saying gently:

"Listen to me, my beloved. I want you to love a man that I wanted to be, but couldn't be. I have but one desire: to love you. I want to make you invincible. I want to prevent you from getting hurt in any way, as I had once hurt your mother.

If I only could, I would obliterate that portion of the brain of Ram, where I taught him how to be a cold blooded assassin without feeling any pain, anguish, or emotions. And then go on with an ordinary life as if nothing had happened. That is the only fear I have.

Natasha, forgive me. It is not you who is confused, but I. I don't know what to believe in. But I know one thing: on one side is the world, and on the other side are you. I chose you, I choose you."

He suddenly realized the fallacy of his entire ideology. His little girl was teaching him now what he could never learn from anyone else. Nobody could ever imagine that this stoic man could feel vulnerable.

The High Lama felt drained. The old wound from the shrapnel in his left lung ached, reminding him of Ram, who once risked his own life to save his. That happened

40

many years ago during the cold war. He felt indebted to Ram.

Deep in his heart he knew that Ram had outgrown his teachings a long time ago; that he had absorbed and internalized all that he had learned from the High Lama, and that he was far ahead of the High Lama himself.

Subconsciously he felt that Ram was a better man than he was, and Ram was worthy of Natasha's love. That had bothered the High Lama the most. It bothered him that Natasha chose Ram and not him, knowing that she and Ram both could be destroyed by the High Lama's invincible circle of power.

Yet deep in his heart he was satisfied with his daughter, because she stood up for her love, and so did Ram. It made the High Lama proud of both of them with a tinge of envy. He did not know what to do, how to handle this situation, and how to finish this unfinished relationship.

His whole being was yearning for release from self deprivation of joy. He wanted to feel simple love, a love beyond ideology, beyond statements and manifestos. He felt like a child who wakes up to play with his toy and for the mother's embrace.

The agony of this deep yearning for simple joy and the anguish of leaving behind what he had lived for all his life, overwhelmed him. The images of his past were dancing before his consciousness, trying to jockey for position.

He felt numb with a sense of relief, like a tired body about to rest its head on a pillow. He did not know where he was. He saw himself involuntarily transported into a different dimension. He fell into a deep trance and went into a mystical regression.

CHAPTER 4

THE
SECRET
SOCIETY

The Invisible Guardians
With No Personal Goals

The High Lama was a member of the secret society that influenced governments and individuals all over the world, without them having knowledge of it. He belonged to the hierarchy of the organization which worked like a finely tuned, well oiled machinery.

The members of this secret society knew the danger of being visible and the danger of having an ego. Any display of an ego could make them a victim of their own organization; and of course, of the world that they have influenced. Ego was their death sentence.

The founders of this secret society had recognized that any label or visibility is a plague. They learned from the history of the Knights Templars, a military order, which became very influential and wealthy particularly in the 13th century.

As soon as the Knights Templars showed arrogance towards kings and religious rulers, they became victims of their own ego. King Philip IV of France, coveting their wealth, brought false charges of sodomy, blasphemy, and heresy against the order. And on Friday the 13th of October 1307 hundreds of Knights Templars in France were simultaneously arrested and then slaughtered. That might be the reason why people say that Friday the 13th brings bad fate.

The founders of the High Lama's secret society realized that visibility of any kind would make them powerless. That was why they stayed invisible, unknown to mankind, yet existing everywhere.

Their organization was made up of people who were cultivated in the philosophy of Pythagoras and Plato. They were immersed in the Vedic principles of knowing the Self; and educated equally in Sun Tzu's "The Art of War", in the diplomacy of Machiavelli, and in the political strategies of Chanakya.

They were unseen guardians with no personal goals, almost invisible individuals; 'almost', because they were vulnerable to each other.

The High Lama and Ram were brothers again. But in this incarnation they were born not of the same father as they were two thousand years ago, but of the same ideology.

Blood is thicker than water, but ideology is thicker than blood. Brothers turn against brothers for ideology.

Conquering a country doesn't mean a thing. You can conquer a country, but you cannot conquer ideology.

That was why both the High Lama and Ram had chosen to come back on a higher spiral in order to resolve their relationship and pay their karmic debts.

The wise sages say that no conflict in life can be resolved on the same level on which it was created. To see the solution to a problem, one should rise above the level on which the problem had occurred.

Although immersed in the knowing and teaching of this philosophy, the High Lama could not figure out how to solve his own problem.

For the first time in his life he was about to violate the sanctity of this ideology and feel not for others, but for himself. He did not understand nor have any explanation for his feelings. Yet, on the subconscious level he was divinely guided by the mysterious power that is hidden behind every action of a man.

This power is stronger than any purpose or any ideology. You can feel it, but you can't explain it. It is logically unexplainable. Yet it can be perceived by the Higher Self, or immortal soul. The sages call it Karma. The scientists call it the Law of Cause and Effect.

CHAPTER 5

IN THE
WILDERNESS
OF THE MIND

A Mystery of Karmic Evil

It was a mystery how this beautiful petite woman, who exuded all the power of the tantric subtleties of life, had also the strength of a Hercules. Her strength was not made of flesh, sinews, and blood. Her strength was in her heart and mind.

Sitting on the sofa by the window of her downtown waterfront condo, Natasha was thinking in wonderment about what she had achieved.

She had accomplished more than she could have ever imagined. She found herself in the arms of the mighty. She had married the strongest man in the whole universe, Ram Shankar Roy. She had been fathered by the giant, the High Lama. She could match both of them with her mental muscles.

Two months passed by since Natasha and Ram had parted without knowing when or where they would see each other again.

They had been followed and almost trapped in their secret meeting place in London. But they were able to escape via the spiral staircase that led from the back room of the restaurant to the basement of another building, which was connected to the tube station. They took a train to Heathrow airport. From Heathrow the two of them took a cab to Gatwick airport.

After a hurried gentle embrace, Natasha entered security to board the plane. They separated to unite again and to fulfill the dreams which they had the courage to dream thousands of years ago.

Now Natasha had to wait. She knew that her father and her husband loved her deeply. She also knew that both of them would fight for her love, as they had fought for her love thousands of years ago.

For what is time? Time is but an illusion created by our imagination. Whatever we have imagined must come to pass. Every deepest desire-thought must be fulfilled, because these very thoughts control our destiny.

And we cannot get rid of them by suppressing them, because they will haunt us from lifetime to lifetime until they are fully gratified.

That is Karma. And there is no escape from its iron grip. We must be ready to face the problem and work it out until the problem is resolved.

That is the reason why these three characters came back now. They met again not by chance. There is not even a slim possibility for chance in this entire universe.

These three characters came back because their souls urged them to be reborn. Their souls pushed them forward towards their destinies, which they had shaped by their own thoughts and desires thousands of years ago.

Each one of them suffered their own pain and had glimpses of pleasure without knowing what made them do what they had done.

Natasha prayed for a miracle that may bring peace to this endless struggle of egos. From time-to-time she had lost her cool. Worried and terrified by the frequent nightmares, she saw Ram combating the opposition directed by her own father.

Then she was afraid to go back to sleep. She was afraid to see the end of her dream. She did not want any of them to win or to lose. She wanted them both. She loved them both.

Her life and her environment had been drastically changed. Natasha realized that she must also change to survive. She must adjust by changing her frightening expectations into the expectations of happiness.

Yet she must stay vigilant and be on guard, ready to act and take control of any situation that may occur.

And at the same time she must find strength in the inner sanctuary of her heart, the place where she had preserved and safely stored her treasured memories of Ram.

Thinking about Ram, Natasha was sucked into a vortex of blissful memories. She saw herself at the foothills of the Himalayan Mountains where she experienced the height of ecstasy, the union with her soul mate.

The feelings of delight flooded her heart. She felt the fragrances of the smoke and the fire, and, through the misty air of the valley, she heard a dreamy voice of the Guru, the enlightened Master of Ram:

"I join your hands for a good fortune that you may perform your duty as your husband's partner in dharma."

All Natasha's fears vanished. She relived the mystical ceremony of her wedding. She felt happy looking into Ram's penetrating eyes filled with exuberant joy, while he tied the end of her sari with his shawl. It was an ancient symbol of ultimate union, the union for ecstasy, the union that transcends all rituals and all rules.

She saw herself walking with Ram seven times around the sacred fire. She felt uplifted, purified, and cleansed by the fire, and finally becoming one with the fire and the light.

"Am I dreaming, or is it real?" She asked herself.

"Yes, it is real. It did happen to me. And this red thread around my wrist is the evidence of my union with Ram, the evidence that I am his woman. And I shall always be his woman, the woman of the warrior, even till the end of time. I will always have this night under the stars with me."

Natasha, a beautiful, slender goddess of love aching to love, got up from her sofa. She stood by the window for a while aimlessly looking at the haze of the horizon.

Slowly gaining the consciousness of the moment, she straightened up her shoulders, and with the voice that sent shivers to the end of the universe, loudly proclaimed:

"I am the woman of the warrior. My first duty is to Ram."

She knew that following Ram would add uncertainty and danger to her life. But what are uncertainties and danger to a loving heart? She knew that all her struggles would help her change, and develop a defense mechanism in her mind, which would make her stronger and teach her what she needed to learn on this journey of life.

She knew that she would conquer all dragons to find her Ram. Yet the negative thoughts in her mind seemed to win more often than the positive thoughts. It was as if she needed to fight her own self to survive, to stay alive, and even to keep her sanity.

Yet, sometimes even among the brightest expectations, Natasha would suddenly catch herself feeling fearful again, seeing herself in the middle of a dreadful place, distant but familiar, where she was trapped, and was not able to take any action to free herself.

"Oh, these devilish thoughts; here they come again," she said, thinking of Jesus, who was led up into the wilderness by the Spirit to be tempted by the Devil. This mysterious Devil is an illusion and a great lie, created by the world of appearances.

"I wonder how many faces this Devil has?" she asked herself, and smiled, thinking about this Devil as her own defeated faith.

"Is there a way, to erase my past Karma and banish all devilish thoughts forever?" she asked herself silently, and then loudly answered:

"I must find out how to do that." This thought lightened her up and brought feelings of relief.

"What is this mystery of karmic evil all about? Why is it following me from incarnation to incarnation? Why do I allow this pain? Where can I get an anesthetic for this pain? Is there a way to change this evil into good? Is there a way to bring my Ram back to me?"

She knew that Ram would come back; and she would be in his arms. But she was anticipating more than that: something that she had remembered from the past.

She knew that she did not fall in love and marry Ram because he was handsome, powerful, and exciting, but because her karma destined it. She knew him from somewhere in the distant past, which had faded from the world's memory, but not from her heart.

She knew that life is eternal. It never ends and never begins. No connections are new. All connections are renewed connections; even this gaze from her window had a reason behind it. Somewhere deep in her subconsciousness she remembered how she had fallen in love with the sage, who had a secret of eternal youth, a secret of complete conquest from aging. There was something in Ram of that sage that she remembered from the distant past.

Gazing out into the haze of the lake, she did not see the artists creating their paintings. Instead, she saw Ram on the stage creating visions with words, and talking about romance between the heart and the soul.

In that surreal state of mind she felt the intense desire and urge for romance. She invoked her lover by exuding love, bringing seduction into being, and generating that special enchantment, which only a trained courtesan can do. Yet, it was not about seduction; it was about her needs being satisfied and fulfilled. She wanted to take back the sage Agustya in the form of Ram.

What an enchanting, mysterious game this universe plays with us! In the wilderness of our mind we cannot find ourselves because we have to go to our hearts. Then we can see that every passerby in our life was there before, is now, and always will be.

When we meet people and don't know why we like or dislike them, we should always remember that they were in our lives before; and now they have come back to finish some unfinished relationships with us.

Through these mixed feelings in a trancelike state, Natasha entered her heart and saw clearly that there was no danger for either of the men she loved.

She saw that the High Lama could not hurt Ram, as much as he would have liked to for his own survival. And Ram would not touch the High Lama, because he always loved him; and he would never surrender his loyalty to him for any cause or reason.

The High Lama, Natasha, and Ram loved each other. Yet, they could never fully realize the foundation of their feelings. It would take them a whole lifetime to reconcile and to pay the karmic debts of Samudragupta, Urvashi and Agustya.

The king Samudragupta loved and admired his elder brother Agustya. Yet, he stole the kingdom from him and wanted to assassinate him; so he could have his kingdom and have his woman. Yet he loved and worshipped him as reverently, as any wholesome Indian boy would love his elder brother who was next to his own father.

Agustya, the great sage, who found the secret of eternal youth, the secret of life, and the secret of existence, came down as Ram to love Natasha.

He had to return in this incarnation to finish the unfinished kiss, to embrace her, to unite with her, and to offer her back his daughter, without knowing what he had offered.

Yet he paid his karmic debt by giving to his lover what she had dreamed about two thousand years ago: Agustya's daughter.

Natasha caught her own reflection in the mirror across the room and playfully said:

"You better get ready Natasha Roy."

Her deep brown eyes were gleaming. She winked, teasing and flirting, as if the spirit of a beautiful courtesan had entered her body. Still looking at her reflection in the mirror, she lowered her voice and mysteriously whispered: "Tomorrow you are going to conquer Paris."

In her mind she was already in Paris, standing on the stage of a huge concert hall, where she was going to speak. Confidently she glanced at her audience looking for Ram. She saw him sitting in the fourth row. She saw his captivating smile half-lost in his beard and mustache. She saw his eyes beaming with power, arousing, inspiring, and making her eager to perform, to entertain, and to enchant, as she had done thousands of years ago.

Intoxicated by his presence, Natasha ceased to exist. Instead it was Urvashi, a gorgeous courtesan who brought with her a vortex of a dream-like-drama which saturated the air around her with aromas and memories of the unfinished kiss, and a burning desire to fulfill her dreams.

CHAPTER 6

THE
OTHER SIDE
OF THE MOON

Love Tainted With Jealousy

The warmth of an unknown joy mixed with longing, enveloped Natasha's heart. She was bubbling and swelling in expectation of something great that was about to happen. It was not what she usually experienced before a public speaking engagement. Public speaking was natural to her. It was her profession. It was because this time she was going to be announced to her audience with her new name, Natasha Roy; the name which had transformed her into a new woman.

Natasha Maclean did not exist anymore. The adaptation of spirit had taken place. And now she had emerged as a new woman empowered by the spirit of the man of her life, her beloved and her teacher, Professor Ram Shankar Roy. It was a magical feeling. She felt serene and humbled by this experience.

As if in a day dream, Natasha had caught a glimpse of herself on the stage saying the words which she had heard from Professor Roy, when she came for the first time to his class:

"Why are you here today?"

She witnessed herself behind the podium in her favourite white designer suit with the black silk blouse slightly showing above the collar of her fully buttoned jacket. She wore black high heeled stiletto shoes. She heard her own voice saying:

"Nowadays physicists are more confused than ever before in what world they live in, and what reality is real to them. They have many different theories, and many different perceptions about reality that sometimes contradict each other.

We all know how it feels when we struggle to understand the world around us, to define our relationships with each other and with the universe. Why do we want to know all this? It is because the most rewarding thing in heaven and earth is to know who we are.

Why did we come here today? Why do we do the things we do? And what makes us do it? What urges us to go where we have never gone before? What pushes us to the end of that cliff and makes us take that unthinkable last step and fall? And what mysterious power lifts us up, nurses our wounds and makes us ready again for a new journey into the mystery of the unknown?

Ah, what a joy it is to travel this endless path of discovery! It is worth it. Every sleepless night, every grueling step we take; it is worth it; for it is the most rewarding journey of our soul. That is why we are re-incarnated: to explore, to grow, to become more, to become wiser and happier than we have ever been before. And I congratulate every one of you, who is following this path of joy.

You, a wonderful race of scientists, always curious and always eager to find the mechanics of this universe, have been able to plug into the source of all knowledge and find out what sages knew thousands of years ago.

You were forced to explore the realm of metaphysics and to find out the meaning of reality. Yet, you were afraid to admit that your views resemble the teachings of mystics, because you have to be concrete and show the facts. But there are many brave among you who can say as Niels Bohr said in The Copenhagen interpretation:

"There is no deep reality"; or who can say as Walter Heitler, and David Bohm:

"Reality is an undivided wholeness"; or who can say as Eugene Wigner and John von Neumann:

"Consciousness creates reality", which is an exact translation from Sanskrit 'Pragyanaam Brahma', which means 'Consciousness creates'.

There are many other theories about reality, which the New Physicists are trying to deal with. Let us take for example "Reality is an undivided wholeness". You have proved scientifically what was widely used by the masters thousands of years ago. You re-discovered that consciousness is the Creator; and that time and space are just illusion; that the universe is nothing else but an undivided whole; and you and I are included in it.

Now you know the truth. But it is one thing to know the truth, and another thing to accept it as your own, and then live it. I will never forget the moment when I had fully realized my relationship with God or, as you call it, 'an undivided wholeness'. The first time in my life I felt invincible. I felt as if I was sitting on my father's lap, the beloved daughter of a king. My father was the ruler of the universe and his kingdom was my playground. And there was nothing that I couldn't do or couldn't have.

When we truly realize what an undivided wholeness means, we understand that everything and everyone are interconnected. It means that there is no vacuum anywhere and no distance. It means that time and space is just an illusion. It means that you and I don't have reasons to fear or feel helpless because anything we ask for is already on its way to us, even from the ends of the world.

This understanding sets us forever free. It means that nothing and nobody can take it away from us, enslave or harm us. When we understand that we are one with an undivided wholeness, that we are one with the source of all power, all wealth, all health, and all wisdom, we become free. All we need to do is to live this understanding. And we live a miraculous life.

When fear is transformed into courage the prison of the mind opens its doors and the prisoner becomes a free man or woman.

Imagine that your reality has been changed. You are not separate anymore. You are an undivided wholeness. Now you can 'scoop abundance from abundance, yet abundance remains,' as the old treatise says.

Why did you come here today? Why did you choose to be a physicist, a scientist? Did it happen by chance, by accident, or by coincidence? There are no such things. Nobody else but you can design your life. Everything that happens to you happens by your own conscious or unconscious intention through your thoughts, feelings, and emotions, which you accepted as truth and your soul embraced it.

All you need to do is to decide which reality is real for you. And you will have it. As Albert Einstein said:

"I want to know all God's thoughts; all the rest are just details."

Do you also want to know all God's thoughts? If you do: live the understanding that 'the Universe is an undivided wholeness', and all the rest will be just details."

Loud applause awoke her from her reverie and brought Natasha back to her bedroom. She found herself standing at the same spot in front of the mirror. Filled with a deep reverence towards the power of the mind, a magical carrier that all humans possess, but very seldom use for their advantage, Natasha said to herself:

"I had already given my speech before I arrived in Paris. And now it is time for me to go there again. This time I will go to Paris by plane."

She automatically took her shower, styled her hair, and packed her clothes for the trip. Then she made her favourite spiced tea with honey, brought it to the living room, and sipped it slowly, sitting on the white plush sofa facing the lake. The rising sun elevated her heart with the feelings of conquest and joy.

Natasha was looking forward to this trip. She was invited as one of the keynote speakers at the world congress of New Physics in Paris. But there was another keynote speaker with the same last name as Natasha's.

She was Roma Roy. Neither women were in the field of science, but they were masters of the architecture of the mind, which is what the New Physics wants to discover.

It was a televised conference, which made the whole planet earth into her audience. Natasha Roy spoke first. She enjoyed and loved the applause. Feeling at ease, yet intrigued and excited, Natasha was waiting for Roma Roy to come to the stage. She wanted to know who that woman was and how she looked; but when Roma began to speak, Natasha did not hear Roma. Instead she heard Ram Shankar Roy through the sweet voice of this beautiful young woman.

Roma and Natasha were very different in appearance, yet there was a noticeable similarity in their delivery, in their posture, and in the power of conviction that both women possessed.

They were pouring out the wisdom of the ages, stunning the world by the eloquence and depth of knowledge of the human spirit.

Both spoke equally well and made the world realize that imagination is reality, but trapped in time and space. Those were the exact words of Ram, which Roma and Natasha used. Both women's curiosity was so intense that they broke protocol and came to see each other.

There was a tinge of love tainted with a trace of jealousy. Natasha being a more mature woman approached Roma. And Roma knew that her dream was fulfilled. Roma wanted her father to have the love of a woman. Natasha's speech confirmed to Roma that Natasha was that woman; because her father's love was pouring out from the heart of Natasha.

Roma always felt that her father was very lonely. That pained her. Now she felt ecstasy. She forgot where she was. She forgot all customs, rushed down the aisle, and, like a little schoolgirl, embraced Natasha and said:

"You must know my father." Roma's words stunned Natasha, as if somebody had awakened her from a deep dream. But she made an effort to hide her feelings.

"Yes, I know your father," Natasha answered without mentioning his name. Unspoken, everything was said. Both women's curiosity took its course. Natasha said:

"I don't know anything about your father, but I love him. Seeing you, I think I know even less. Why was he hiding you from me? You don't light a candle and hide it under a bushel."

Roma answered with a question: "Why wasn't I at your wedding?" They both wanted to have the answers that only Ram could give. But Ram was not there.

They left the conference hall eager to find out more about each others lives. All they knew is that they loved and honored the same man, who had been their teacher.

Without any preamble Roma began her story: "When Ram's father died, Ram had just finished high school. One day he went out with a bunch of boys and girls to the local park. One of the neighbors saw them and reported him to the girl's family. Ram was a close friend of the brother of that girl.

When later Ram came to meet his friend, the whole family accosted him and said that Ram had ruined their daughter's life by taking her out. Now nobody would marry her. They insisted that Ram should take that responsibility for the rest of his life. They questioned his honour and the honour of his family.

Ram was trapped. He was young. He had never faced this situation before. He was a revolutionary in spirit. Ram never even touched this girl. There was not even a trace of love from either side. But the girl's parents saw a good catch. Ram was from a good family. In India it counts a lot. They also figured out that he was easy to attack.

He had just completed his father's funeral ceremony. His head was shaved and his hair had not even started to grow back. He was very emotional. He felt that he had to save this young woman from being dishonored. They made him believe that he was responsible. They manipulated him to marry this girl. They even went to visit Ram's family, portrayed him as a villain, and said:

"Your son has given our daughter his word. We need your consent."

Ram's mother was shocked. She said: "I have just become a widow. I am very vulnerable. My son is not ready to get married. He is too young and doesn't have a profession to support his family. If you and your daughter are willing to wait, it will be good for my son. However, let me tell you, you don't have my agreement, but I will disown my son if he will not keep his word."

The girl's family could not wait. They were anxious to get rid of their daughter at the lowest possible cost to the highest bidder, because they considered her a burden. They manipulated Ram into marriage.

He lived the life of misery, humiliated by the family because he could not properly provide for his wife. He was also rejected by his own mother who needed his financial support.

Yet, he never stopped studying. Somehow he struggled through college, but never gave up his vision. Nobody knew how he had managed. He used to go away for weeks and come back, and still get his percentage of attendance in college to sit for exams."

Roma stopped for a moment and, looking straight into Natasha's eyes, whispered:

"My father did not want to have a child. I am just an accident of destiny. He even told me that.

When I was one year old, my mother left me and my father for another man. My father brought me up with the help of a woman who had her own children. I have lived the life of a Cinderella, yet the entire family was supported by my father.

I felt angry with my father. He used to come to pick me up; and I use to wait for him by the window with my blanket. He always lived separate. He used to teach me how to cook, clean, write, and read. The best I know I learned from him.

Who said a father could be busy and not pay attention to his child? My education was completed before I went to college. He taught me to believe in magic. And this belief brought me to the point where I am today. It brought me to this moment of meeting you. I don't even know how I should address you."

Natasha was quiet. She did not want to interrupt, or suggest, or help Roma to figure out her feelings. Overwhelmed by this unexpected meeting with Ram's daughter, Natasha was experiencing some unknown feelings. Yet they seemed familiar as if these feelings were inherited by her soul from her previous incarnations. They were the feelings of unfulfilled motherhood, which came back to be re-lived.

Natasha felt a sensation of helplessness as she was caught up in a tornado of love. It was an unexplainable love that every woman has buried deep inside. It only surfaces when she holds her child for the first time in her arms, pressing against her bosom after an exhausting battle with her body to give birth.

She felt the same way looking at Roma's face. She wanted to embrace her and hold her tight against her breasts and give her the warmth of a mother that she had never experienced. Then both of them would become complete; would become whole.

Her heart ached for that touch, and that embrace, and that gentle voice of a powerful daughter telling her:

"I would like you to be my mother."

But it did not happen. Yet the connection was made. This connection comes naturally. When souls unite, it is like a flash of lightening in the sky.

Roma was afraid of rejection. She had a wounded heart on which she had put a band aid of cynicism, fortified with skepticism. Natasha felt it. Yet she did not make any move to ease her pain. She just listened silently, knowing that it would take a miracle to heal

CHAPTER 7

IN LOVE
WITH THE SAME
MAN

A Mental Storm

Transcending the Logical Mind

Natasha felt she was not in Paris anymore. She looked at Roma and had a queasy sensation that Roma was not what she appeared to be. She wanted to embrace her. Yet she didn't want to do that. Natasha didn't know what she wanted to do. She just wanted to love her and not get involved; the same way she felt, when she first saw Ram Shankar. She felt that she knew him; yet, she never saw him before that day. She felt that she belonged to him and that he was just waiting for her return.

This young woman, Roma Roy, was giving her the same feeling, and she wanted no more attachments. Yet she wanted to give her the love that she was waiting to pour out for centuries. Natasha knew that this was not normal At the same time Natasha wanted with all her heart to feel this magnificent woman's love.

A dim light seemed to surround her. She felt she had entered into a vortex and was pulled into a distant past. She tried to hold onto the moment, but her mental grip was not strong enough.

The whirlpool of the past sucked her back into the arms of her lover sage at a time before the great Buddha enraptured the world with his philosophy. Liberated from the clutches of this three dimensional world, she found herself not as Natasha, not as the world saw her now.

She was a mother. She was a mother for a few moments. She felt the sweetest pain of all, the pain of motherhood; the joy, which a goddess envies. She gave birth to the most beautiful girl in the midst of total seclusion and knowing that her lover, the great sage Agustya was executed by the King Samudragupta just to win her love. And she handed over the great Agustya's seed to the safekeeping of his executioner under certain conditions.

Now this same girl seems to be putting on her 'ankle bells' and trying to match her mother. Now this same girl wants to embrace her, but does not know why she wants to do it.

She felt that her whole life: the past, the present, and the future had diminished into an everlasting now and an eternal here.

Both of them were going through this mental storm and both of them did not realize what was happening to them. Both these beautiful and powerful women loved the same man; and both were overprotective of Ram Shankar, but with a difference.

One was his daughter, who was his anchor to reality; and the other was his consort and his beloved wife, who was his journey into mysticism and fantasy.

They, without rhyme or reason, wanted to express to each other their accumulated thoughts:

"Ma, my beautiful Ma, I just wanted to say: I love you."

And the other:

"My daughter, my beautiful daughter, I never saw you, but I, for two thousand years, have carried the unfinished kiss; and I want to kiss you, and tell you that I love you."

The lack of courage to express these thoughts was tormenting both of them. While they were sitting in the crowded sidewalk café, the sensation of a strange bond between them was growing stronger, as if an emotional umbilical cord held them together with an unexplainable power that was beyond the understanding of the logical mind.

All of a sudden the weather had changed. The wind from the North brought heavy clouds followed by heavy thoughts which have been roaming the universe for two thousand years, looking for the right moment to release themselves in a dream-like ecstasy.

The wind brought chills to Natasha's spine. She closed her eyes, took a deep breath, and tried to shake off this unpleasant feeling.

But the wind was a hungry lover and would not let her go. She surrendered. The wind propelled her to a different dimension beyond the bounds of time.

All of a sudden she felt a weird weakness, as if there was no blood left in her body to feed her heart. She saw a small mud hut and a woman lying on a wooden bed with a new born baby pressed to her breasts.

"Who is this woman?" She thought, trying to see her face; then realizing that it was her own face. It was she who was dying in the puddle of blood after giving birth to her daughter.

She suddenly remembered who she was. She was Urvashi, the most beautiful courtesan of the Golden Age of India, who refused to accept the love of the king of that land, Samudragupta, because her heart was already given to a sage from the forest, the great mystic Agustya.

After the night of a heavenly union with her beloved Agustya, he suddenly vanished from the face of the earth without knowing that Urvashi was carrying the seed of his love in her womb. In agony and pain Urvashi gave birth to Sangita and died, without fulfilling her dreams or experiencing the joys of motherhood.

Still feeling the pangs of unsatisfied motherly love, Natasha opened her eyes. And, as if it was an answer to her prayers, there was Roma Roy sitting across the table with an expression of love and fear frozen in her beautiful eyes.

"Is it possible that Roma is my Sangita that came back to me through the womb of another woman?" thought Natasha looking at her face, which was a replica of Ram in a feminine form. In fact she was more adamant, more emphatic, and more expressive than Ram, who always subdued those tendencies in himself.

"Is everything all right?" asked Roma worryingly, trying not to call Natasha by her name. "Would you like something to drink?"

"A cup of mint tea would be great," said Natasha thinking that Roma was not just a woman, who looked like Ram. From the moment she had met her she knew that their connection was not of this life only. She knew that no connections in life are of this life only.

Natasha knew that Roma belonged to her. Roma was her heart. Roma was the woman that she gave birth to two thousand years ago in her womb impregnated by her great sage, Agustya. At that time she did not want Roma to dance and amuse kings. She wanted Roma to carry on the power of Agustya. Today Agustya is Ram.

She felt that Roma was her own, somewhere someplace in a distant time. The womb that gave Roma the entrance to this world was only a gateway to meet Natasha.

That was why Roma did not have any bond with her mother. And as such for the first time Roma also felt a yearning for closeness. Roma did not know in her life what a mother's love was; or what a connection with a mother could be. It was not because of her mother's fault, but because of Roma's mental state. That was why the connection could never be made.

The whole journey of Roma's soul was to come and meet this moment; and only then her real life could start. She could not understand it, but she felt it. And the feeling was so intense that it was driving her mad.

Roma was a very mature young woman. She understood the world. She was a powerful thinker and a very detached person too. Yet she also felt an intense attachment. She did not know two things: why she was feeling this way; and how she could express her feelings.

Roma's relationship with her father was unique. Ram felt that his connection with his daughter was something from the past. But Roma was unaware of this. For her it was difficult to understand how her father could be so different from her friends' fathers. She used to ask Ram:

"Why are you not like every one else? You are the only one in the whole neighborhood who is a vegetarian. You don't watch sports and do grocery shopping every Thursday or Friday. Why don't you hang out in the bars like other fathers do? Why don't you buy beer and invite

people for barbeques? Why don't you have a pair of shorts
and a baseball cap? You don't even have shorts. Why are
you not like every one else? People are talking behind
your back, wondering who you are."

And if Ram would offer to take Roma grocery
shopping, she would usually say:

"No, we will go and pick up things when we need
them."

She was brought up that way. And she lived that
way. She had a very strong connection with her father, but
she never understood it. And Ram knew that.

He never wanted to have any children. Yet when
he got Roma, he knew that it was his Karma to bring her
up.

Natasha never had a child. But now looking at
Roma she felt the pangs of motherhood in her breasts for
the first time. And yet i was not for a baby. It was for a
grown up woman.

Natasha was afraid what it might lead to. At the
same time there was a yearning for an embrace. She
wanted to distance herself. And yet some unseen
mysterious force pulled her towards Roma.

Sometimes we feel that urge, when we see
somebody, perhaps a stranger we don't even know, but the
urge is there and the fear is there also. It seems foolish for
the mind, yet some unknown power makes us act in a way
that looks strange to our intellect.

This is very important to understand, so we will
be aware and will not miss the treasure that is waiting for
us, and a magical gift that we were born to receive.

CHAPTER 8

APPARITION

IN

PARIS

Yearning for a Lover's Embrace

Natasha flew straight from Toronto in a direct flight with Air Canada to Paris. She was running out of time to give her lecture. From the de Gaulle airport she took a limousine to the conference centre without stopping at the hotel

     Then she felt compelled to stay a bit longer to hear this magnificent young woman with the same last name as hers, giving a talk after her.

     It was an exciting and moving moment in her life. She met her daughter; yet her daughter did not know that she had met the mother of another lifetime.

She was Sangita, a princess who was forbidden to dance two thousand years ago. Now she was dancing with new dancing bells; and these dancing bells were not tied to her ankles anymore, but to the Venus center in her throat, through which her voice was reverberating. With every syllable and with every word that she uttered, Natasha heard the heart of Ram. Roma was the heart of Ram. She was totally engulfed by his love.

All the great scientists of the world sat and listened to her most profound lecture. Science and art were dancing on the stage with her jockeying for position: who is going to lead, and who is going to follow. The science of Newton had become the science of antiquity. Now Quantum Physics is exploring the realm of metaphysics to find the mystery of reality.

But the real mystery was in the heart of Natasha. She could not overcome the idea that she had met this woman; and yet she did not know her. In that exhausting moment of her life, exhausting, because her heart wanted to know more than her brain could offer, she was driven to her hotel.

Natasha loved every moment. She loved conquering all the scientists' hearts. She loved the applause. But all that was not enough for her. She wanted the touch of her man, the touch of his chest against her bare breasts. She wanted to live in his arms forever.

The Nobel laureates' applause was exciting, but not satisfying. There was no contentment. It was giving comfort to her ego, not to her heart.

The limousine glided to the main entrance of the InterContinental Le Grand Hotel The doorman welcomed Natasha into a splendid lobby dressed in luxurious wood, marble, and gold. Passing through the doorway she nodded, smiled gently to the doorman, and moved towards the reception desk.

Natasha had reserved a deluxe room with a view of the Opera House. But before she had reached the reception desk, the bell captain was already on his way to greet her:

"Bonsoir, madam," he said and gave her the key.

"I have not yet checked in," Natasha said.

"Oh yes, you have," he answered with a polite smile, and continued:

"All arrangements have been made, Mrs. Roy. The room you have booked was not available, so we have upgraded your room to the Prestige Suite."

"That is lovely," she said. "I am sure I will enjoy it. But how did you find out my name?"

"I saw you on TV today; and I heard you speak. You have inspired me, Mrs. Roy. So I decided to take philosophy next semester at the Sorbonne."

Happy with the generous tip, the bell captain respectfully bowed and left, quietly closing the door behind him.

Finally Natasha was able to take off her high heeled shoes and walk around her suite. It was beautiful:

warm and cozy, decorated with gorgeous pictures from the world of opera and ballet. She admired the luxurious dark oak bed, complemented by crisp white linens and a designer throw. There were two bathrooms in her suite dressed in marble and gold.

She enjoyed a long hot shower, styled her hair, and decorated her face as she had learned in the Himalayan village from the local girls. She put her silk black evening gown on, as if she would be going out to the Opera House, or preparing herself for a very special event in her life.

It became her ritual: to get dressed up every night, as if she had a date with Ram. Fully dressed she sat on the sofa by the window in the lounge area of her suite and witnessed herself sitting there. Every object in the suite was alive, promising comfort and pleasure. There was intimacy and seduction in the air. She was in Paris.

Champagne was on the ice; it was the favourite of Ram, "Dom Perignon", named after the French monk who worked for years developing and producing this provocative sparkling wine.

The bottle was opened, as if some invisible hand did it for her. It was fresh; the bubbles were about to burst out.

"How can it be?" she thought, but she loved it. She poured the champagne into the glass and, holding it lightly between her middle and ring fingers, sipped it…

She almost heard the voice of Ram bursting through the bubbles and wetting her cheeks. Her heart was pounding.

Natasha got up from the sofa and went to the window. She could see the Opera House; she could see the Seine River; she could see in the distance the Eiffel Tower lit up against the sky.

Ram mentioned that he had stayed here; that was why Natasha had chosen this hotel. She wanted to experience the atmosphere Ram had experienced. It was her way of entering his spirit and being with him.

He told her that he used to go for a walk down the river near the Eiffel Tower. He told her about the lovers along the banks of the river kissing and embracing. He told her about the greatest romantic in the world, after whom this city was named. He had violated all the traditions and all the laws, and gave up his kingdom, Troy, for a mad illicit love. He was Paris.

The soft blue sky engulfed her yearning for union with Ram. Night was welcoming her to bed, but the bed would be empty without Ram.

Natasha loved this man. She had loved him in the forest, in the hut, in the makeshift bed where she made love to him and conceived Sangita.

She stood by the window and looked out at the sky for some time. She heard many stories from Ram about this romantic city located at the crossroads of Europe.

Natasha had been to Paris before, but now she was looking at everything around her with Ram's eyes.

"I shall come back to this hotel with my lover," she thought looking at the famous Opera House.

She saw herself walking in the streets of Paris with Ram, holding hands, stopping and kissing in the middle of the street; then taking a whole day of pleasure in the Louvre, and browsing through the famous boutiques of the Rue du Faubourg St-Honoré.

She remembered Ram's exuberant animated face, when he talked to her about his first visit to Paris, and that his life has never been the same since. She wondered how that first visit affected his life. Thinking about that, she went into a trance.

She saw Agustya, the great sage who could have been the emperor, looking right into her face and saying:

"Urvashi, I have failed you as a lover. I gave you my love. I gave you the ecstasy and joy of a lover that no woman had ever experienced before; but I did not finish loving you. Your heart is still longing for me."

In that trancelike state she awoke and yearned for the grip of Ram around her body. She felt the embrace...

There was nobody in the room, but she felt the embrace. She felt his arms holding her from the back and touching her breasts. She inhaled a subtle sweet aroma of the "Orient Express" tobacco, mingled with the scent of Grey Flannel, the French Cologne that was the trade mark of Ram. Natasha felt the arousing fragrance of Ram all around her; and she almost went into an ecstasy.

Ram looked into her eyes and asked:

"Were you waiting for me?"

Natasha was speechless. She thought she was imagining. No, she wasn't, because she felt his embrace. It was not Agustya. It was Ram. Ram was holding her. She could not understand how Ram could do that; yet she knew that he could open closed doors and walk through walls invisible to the human eye. He could do anything, because he was Ram.

CHAPTER 9

DO NOT UNDRESS, MY LOVE

The Romance

That Can Never Be Fulfilled

Ram left the hotel before dawn unnoticed by anyone, as invisible as he had arrived. Through his contacts in Europe, Ram made all the arrangements for that night. Nobody knew about his plans except the High Lama, who secretly monitored every single step of Natasha and Ram.

The High Lama was astonished and amazed by the intensity and power of their love that knew no fear. It seemed that the union of their souls had created an unseen shield of protection around them, and made them invincible. They were willing to live for each other; not to die, but to live, no matter what. And there was no power in heaven or on earth that could prevent or stop them from being together.

When Ram entered the room, he saw Natasha's slender silhouette standing by the window. Her eyes were closed; her head was lifted up slightly, as if she was listening to the inner music shaped by her desires.

She stood motionless, filled with a scorching flame of longing, waiting for her lover. She became a living magnet charged by her desires pulsating through space. The blissful anticipation of union was so certain that she could sense Ram's presence around her.

She heard Ram's voice calling her name. She felt his energy flooding the room...

Ram embraced Natasha gently from the back; and before she became conscious of what had happened, or made any noise, or shouted in excitement; he turned her around, and sealed her mouth with a long passionate kiss.

She moaned, melted in his arms, and instantly surrendered to her mighty lover. He was holding her in his strong arms. He was there. He was real...

It felt like the whole city was being inflamed. Ram picked Natasha up, swung her, carried her towards the sofa, and put her on his lap.

The memory of this moment was locked in his heart with all its ecstatic sounds and fragrances.

All of a sudden Ram became aware of the droning sound of the plane, gliding towards the sunrise. Ram took a deep breath and opened his eyes. Feeling the heat of the ecstasy of the memory, he had a sip of water and let his body relax. For a moment, which seemed like eternity, he experienced in his mind last night again.

Romance was oozing out from Natasha's eyes. She brought her lips close and whispered in his ear:

"Let this night never end."

She took Ram's pipe, which he always carried with him, and filled it herself with his aromatic "Orient Express" tobacco. Feeling intoxicated with Ram's presence, she watched him light his pipe, while trying to calm down his heightened senses.

But nothing could stop Natasha. She started to move her body gently in Ram's arms. A sudden transformation took place: a seductive gorgeous courtesan had awakened in her from a dreamless sleep. She brought her heavenly beauty to earth and entered this stage of life.

She stormed this stage with the ecstasy of love, the ecstasy of union, and the ecstasy of the ultimate clasp of silence. She brought the excitement to its ultimate peak. It was a dance of love that was waiting for two thousand years to express itself now.

Ablaze with the agonizing fire of lust, she made the first attempt to undrape her body. Slowly, she began to pull down the left shoulder of her silk evening gown. Her ivory skin vibrating with a magnetic joy was exposed.

With all his mighty strength Ram struggled to contain himself. He was on the edge, yet he wanted to prolong the rapture with foreplay.

"Let's have some champagne," he said and stretched his arm to pull the bottle by the neck from the ice bucket. He took a sip straight from the bottle, and passed it to Natasha. She took it from Ram's hands, pressed it against her luscious lips, and tilted her head back to drink. Ram saw her neck; her ivory breasts, and whispered:

"Natasha, the heavens have not seen such beauty. What a shame, as I will not share this beauty even with God."

Ram looked at Natasha and lowered his eyes. The uncontained fire was threatening to burn to cinders his frightened senses.

"Do not undress, my love," asked Ram. "Let me hold your face and look into your eyes. Look and fill my heart with your beauty."

"You are pouring poetry from your soul," whispered Natasha. She reached for the scratch pad and pen, which were on the lamp table, passed them to Ram and said:

"Close your eyes and write. Feel me, and write."

Her body was gently gyrating with the music that was faintly playing in the background; from side to side, totally dissolving, totally merging with Ram's body and soul, feeling the oneness, feeling union, and feeling total bliss.

While he was writing, Natasha was sitting on his lap with her eyes closed, heightened by every movement of Ram's pen. Natasha knew that a great piece of poetry was taking birth, while she was exalted in rapture on the lap of her lover.

Then, there was no feeling. Feeling appeared as separation. They reached the eye of the storm of their passion, and entered into the stillness of the eye. While a storm was raging in the rapture of their kisses and embraces in the vortex of love, they were still in union, while their bodies played.

Then, there was silence. The storm ended. They slumbered for a few minutes into oblivion in each other's arms, after the loving, to get relief from the clutches of ecstasy.

Awakened as a new blossom, Natasha looked at Ram, gave her coquettish giggle, and said:

"I would love to know what you scribbled in the dark."

Ram cleared his throat, while giving a quick survey of the curvature of Natasha's slender body profiled under her silk evening gown, and began to read with his gravelly voice:

> *"Do not undress, my love.*
> *Let me look into your eyes*
> *And make love to you.*
>
> *Do not kiss me with passion.*
> *Look into my eyes,*

And pour your passion into my soul;
And let the ecstasy stay.

Let me hold your face and look...
Look and fill my heart
With your beauty.

Let us separate
To realize our love,
To feel our constant union.

Give me your hand.
Let me touch you with my eyes.
Let me burn the world
With the fire of love;

And cleanse all dullness,
And make this world the place of joy,
The infinite joy of divine love.

Come, hold me, and kiss my chest.
And burn me into cinders
With your love.
And raise me, like a phoenix,
Reborn of pure ecstatic love.

Love me,
And teach me,
How to love."

The monotonous sound of the plane gliding towards the sunrise was comforting and promising pleasant dreams; but Ram did not want to fall asleep. He wanted to stay awake and revel in the ecstasy of feeling the joys of love for the first time.

He just loved his woman. A random thought of her was translated into poetry. Ram realized that poetry was the only way he could express the love that was welling up in his heart. He wanted to compile a book of verses and name it "Natasha". His search for life had been accomplished.

"Am I dreaming, or is this real?" was a question that Ram asked himself many times without looking for an answer.

Ram was a dreamer. He wanted the world to be a beautiful place with no borders, with no separation between people, with no wars, hunger or pain. He always dreamed how a world like this would look. He saw the faces of the people around him glowing with happiness and joy.

Now, thinking back, he understood why he was dreaming about one peaceful and harmonious world, and why it was so important for him to have it.

Childhood and adolescence was a blur in Ram's mind. The memory bank of his adolescence seems to have been frozen by his soul and kept dormant. He did not want to remember. It was a paradox.

At age seven he was packed off to an English speaking boarding school. Yet, he did not speak a word of English. It was the best school in India. His school buddies were the super elite. They admired Ram. They wanted to be his friends. He instinctively stayed far from them. He knew, even with a child's mind, that the economic divide between him and them was too wide to maintain his dignity.

Ram's father was an affluent and renowned man. Yet he believed that by giving his son the economic luxury that his classmates enjoyed, would amount to his son's decadence and destruction.

Ram's mother was a beautiful woman. She loved her son deeply. Yet she never cuddled, embraced, or kissed him. So, he would often wonder how it would feel if he put his head on her lap and she stroked his hair, as she did to his younger brother, Akash.

So, at the start of his summer holidays, after Ram bid his rich school buddies goodbye, and came home, he would happily go and play marbles with the boys in the slums. He felt comfortable in their homes; and their parents treated him as one of them. There he had his slum aunt, slum uncle, slum grandfather, and grandmother. They loved him. They gave him the affection that he had never experienced in his own home.

He just realized that he did not know what a home was until Natasha walked into his life; and he also knew it was all necessary to strengthen him and to make him invincible.

Ram realized that he was tested and tried by the universe many times over, until the dross of the old limitations and habits vanished; and he was able to find his calling and realize his mission.

That was the time when the High Lama walked into Ram's life and became his mentor, his guide, and more than his own father. He took Ram under his wing and gave him the purpose and the vision of a new world without borders, without suffering and pain.

Ram knew that the path he had chosen was dangerous. It was a narrow path suited only for the daring. And he wanted to be daring. He wanted to leave his mark on this planet and build a New World governed by Love and Beauty.

From that time onward all his fights in life were for love and more love. His urge for learning and understanding others made Ram look for answers in different religions. And all religions were teaching love. They were like rivers, which had the same destination, the ocean.

Now Ram was ready. He was ready to give and to receive, and to flood this world with so much love, that there would be no room left for sadness, fear, and pain.

More than that, now he was given an opportunity to understand how to give without being rewarded for anything he did; and how to receive the ocean of love, dissolve in it, become one, feel total unity and bliss…

The dream of Ram's childhood, the greatest desire of all, to love and to be loved was fulfilled.

CHAPTER 10

INTERTWINED
IN ONE
DREAM

Revelation of the Encryption of Karma

Strange as it was, Natasha did not feel any sense of emptiness, or sadness after Ram reluctantly left her arms and vanished in the darkness of the night.

Her hungry senses, the shadows of the unfinished kisses were gratified; and her soul, free of the past karma, was released to move on to higher delights that were waiting.

She felt contented, as if she had arrived at a destination of her choice. Fully aware of this new experience, she was able to recognize that her present life is not all, but is a part of all; her yesterday, today, and tomorrow is but a splendid, never-ending Eternity.

This realization was magical. Her consciousness changed: she was able to feel the thrill of the moment, and to look forward without fear.

A mysterious smile appeared on her beautiful face. She was no longer terrified or worried about the outcome of the battle between the High Lama and Ram.

She was expecting a miracle. She knew that her prayer was already answered, and there was no need to strain herself. She knew that her life had been changed; and she was going to enjoy her journey, even though a seeming detour was in front of her.

"I am blessed and free," she thought.

"I love and I am loved. What else is there to want? Of course, I want to be surrounded with opulence and beauty, because I appreciate and enjoy it.

But what is there that I want to take with me wherever I'll go?"

The image of Ram appeared before Natasha. She did not want to think anymore or to ask any questions. All her thoughts became redundant in front of Ram's dark magnetic eyes, filled with exultation of a never ending orgasm.

In that euphoric state that knows no rest, no form, and no dimension, she journeyed from present to past; from a romantic Paris to an enchanting forest; from a luxury hotel to a humble cottage; from the arms of Ram to the arms of Agustya; from lifetime to lifetime along the endless path of refined memories and gratifying delights.

"I want to feel all I can feel," she thought.

"I do care for things, but they are of no use to me without my lover. I want to live in his arms. I want to feel the perpetual ecstasy of the unfinished kiss. I want my life to be a living legend of romance. I care to live and to love…"

The power of her passion aroused the universe itself. It stopped. But just for an instant that created a thunder. That thunder destroyed existence. It merged her past, present, and future into a perpetual blissful Now.

All that she had ever experienced or felt merged and blended into one unique essence, the warm essence of her soul. And the universe helplessly inhaled that essence, and recorded it in the Book of Life.

Our every action, thought, and feeling creates our karma and records it in a Sacred Book. That is what we remember; and that is what we take with us wherever we go. We take our thoughts and our feelings.

Turning the pages encrypted by karma in the Book of Life, Natasha went into ecstasy. She wanted to stay awake and feel her Ram, and to see his half closed eyes, and to hear his soft dreamy voice whispering in her ears: "Do not undress, my love…"

When they were still engrossed in the most romantic interlude, and were in total bliss, Natasha said to Ram:

"You are more than everybody could see. You are travelling the world, giving lectures and seminars. I know that it is not for money. What are you doing Ram, and why?"

He was still an enigma for Natasha. Something was there behind the surface, something she was trying to reach and to understand. She knew that one day she would find out who her lover was.

Ram kept quiet, and then said:

"I cannot lie to you, even when I need to lie. Please forgive me, my love that I did not tell you all about myself.

I have a secret mission in my life. It is a noble mission. It shall make this world a happier and a richer place. But the less you know, the better off you will be."

"Why?" she asked. "Is it dangerous?" "Yes," said Ram. He paused for a moment, and reluctantly continued:

"It is dangerous to be on this path: there are powerful forces against us; the opposition is watching every step we make.

Natasha, I don't want you to get involved in this part of my life."

Ram finished, moved his body down, and put his face between Natasha's breasts.

"Let me rest here for a while. This is my hiding place, my Nirvana."

She pressed him to her heart, caressed his hair, inhaling the arousing scent of his body. They were silent. The whole world stood still absorbing this moment.

"Tell me more, my darling," she asked. "Please tell me more."

Ram raised his head, looked into Natasha's eyes, and then kissed her.

"All I can tell you, my beloved: remember this kiss," he said. He put his head back between Natasha's breasts, closed his eyes, and whispered:

"This moment is all we have. Remember this moment."

"Oh, Ram! I will remember every moment with you. I remember even the dream like memory of my past existence, when you picked me up on your horse and we eloped from my father's home; I remember when you asked me to be your woman; I remember the moon, and the sky, and the stars, and the whole universe as our witnesses."

"You are my universe, my Natasha. I am blessed to hold you in my arms."

And before Ram finished his sentence, he had descended into a slumber, taking Natasha with him into a dream, or reality, who knows... But in a short time they lived a long life on a different planet.

Natasha saw Ram working there. That planet was very far from the earth and totally unknown to Natasha. There were five hundred different nations living there. And all of them were suffering because the nearby planet was extracting all their natural resources.

At the same time that nearby planet was encouraging these five hundred nations to stay separate from each other in order to prevent revolt.

Natasha saw her Ram plotting to unite these five hundred nations with a common purpose in order to free them from the dependency of that planet.

"This is so typical of Ram," she thought in her dream.

"Why does he always have to right some wrong? Why not leave people alone and let them find out what is good for them without interfering?"

Feeling that Ram was in danger, Natasha moved in her sleep. Her movement awoke Ram. They looked at each other and smiled, happy to be in each others arms.

Ram left before dawn, covered by the dark blanket of the night. Natasha stood by the window for a while listening to the sounds coming from the street. There was nothing out of the ordinary. She knew that Ram was safe; and, probably far away from the hotel, on his way back to his mission.

Yet his spirit was still there. She heard Ram's soft voice saying:

"I am with you. It doesn't matter where I am, I am always with you. Feel me."

She felt him.

"Come closer," she asked, whispering gently in Ram's invisible ear.

"Hold me and lull me to sleep."

He smiled, kissed her, and said:

"You are beautiful, my Natasha; and you are strong, stronger than your father and your husband combined. You are the woman of a warrior. Know that I am always with you. Turn around; let me hold you."

She turned around and felt his warm breath caressing her neck. Intertwined in one dream they merged into one consciousness, where there is no distance and no time.

PART TWO

CONFESSION

CHAPTER 11

THE
CALL
OF DESTINY

Courage

Amidst a Fast Unfolding Drama

Natasha could not believe her ears when she picked up the phone and heard her father's voice. She was stunned. The High Lama had never called her before. She heard him saying in his powerful, yet gentle voice:

"Natasha, I called to tell you that I love you. It is my responsibility as a father to protect you. You might not like it, but I will still do it until my last breath.

You understand that I know every step you make. I know that you and Ram had met in Paris. Ram risked his life to see you."

Natasha's heart trembled; she couldn't wait any longer. Sensing danger, she interrupted her father and asked him in a shaking voice:

"Why are you calling me papa? What happened to Ram?"

"I called to find out if you have heard anything from Ram after that night in Paris? Anything, Natasha," he added, slightly raising his voice.

"It is very important. I know how you feel, but you should trust me."

"Papa, tell me what happened to Ram," she repeated; then paused and, after gaining back her confidence, she firmly said:

"I need to know. All this time I was waiting. I feared that you might call…"

"You don't need to fear me, or think that I am against Ram," the High Lama replied in a very kind gentle tone; then he continued in a firmer slightly louder voice:

"I called to let you know that Ram's plane had disappeared together with Ram and his pilot over the Himalayan Range. And all my efforts to find Ram within the last six months have ended without success.

Natasha, I don't know if Ram is alive or dead. I know that you love him. And I will do everything possible to find him. This is a father's promise to his daughter."

The High Lama's voice was filled with compassion and love. There was a strong feeling in Natasha's heart that the High Lama was telling the truth; but she did not want to risk believing him. Yet, she felt his love and concern for her.

A moment later, chilled and shivering, feeling trapped and being at the mercy of a powerful force that was beyond her control, Natasha came back to her senses. She realized that her father was still on the phone, silently waiting for her answer.

She gathered all her strength, and looking inside her heart said: "I have a feeling that something has happened to Ram since I saw him last time in Paris. Perhaps there was an accident of some kind, because he never called me after his mysterious appearance that night in the Grand Hotel. I haven't talked to him since that night. Yet, my heart tells me that he is alive."

Then she added in a voice that proclaimed her confidence and power and made even the mighty High Lama astonished:

"This is not the end of the world. Nothing can separate Ram from me; nothing, including you, papa."

As the High Lama suspected, Natasha did not know where Ram was. Yet he had a reason for giving his daughter this horrible news. He wanted to find out how much she was informed.

He knew his daughter. He knew that she loved Ram with all her heart. He needed to feel her reaction to figure out if Natasha and Ram were still in contact with each other.

The High Lama was the most influential man on the globe today. Once a king and an emperor that conquered many lands, he could not conquer the heart of a woman he loved.

He had many wives and many lovers, yet he loved only one woman. And that woman was just a courtesan. And yet he wanted her.

She couldn't love him. She gave a promise to love a sage. And now in this incarnation the same woman had also given the promise of greatness to love the same man. It was a similar situation being replayed out again.

In this incarnation the same woman came to the High Lama's home, not as a courtesan, but as his daughter. And the father's love was not as important to her as the love of the virtual enemy of her father. Yet that undeclared and yet discovered enemy was trained by her father.

In this lifetime Samudragupta and Agustya were not brothers, but almost as a father and a son. This time the son was trained to be a fighter and a warrior by the father, who was also designed to destroy his son, when his son would reach the peak of power and accomplish his goals.

Yet right now Ram holds the strings to this man's life, who is a virtual father to him. Ram holds the heart of Natasha, the High Lama's only love.

In Natasha the High Lama saw his own charm, his own genes, and his own power. He was not sure whether

Ram loved his daughter, or used Natasha to control him. And neither was Ram sure whether the High Lama used Natasha to eliminate him.

Ram could not believe for a moment that Natasha would hurt him. But his instinct, his own training, his left brain acted. He remembered in a quiet trance how women would poison men in the time of Agustya and Samudragupta. They were called poison-women, or Vishkanyas.

During the time of Agustya and Samudragupta these women were prepared from childhood to become assassins. They were given the most vicious poison in small doses to grow in them. And they also were trained to become the most charming courtesans and the greatest lovers in the world. Any man could make love to this woman only once. And after that love he was poisoned. And he would never wake up from the sleep of union.

They were enchanting assassins. Ram saw the metaphor of the same situation. He knew, of course, he was not poisoned, yet the metaphor of Vishkanyas always raised its ugly head in his mind. And often, when he thought about Natasha, he thought of the most intricate political tactics.

The High Lama could not catch up to him. Ram was a genius in maneuverability. Maneuverability was his instinct for survival that he brought with him to this incarnation from two thousand years ago; and it had stayed with him.

Now before every character there is a big question. Every character is torn apart.

The High Lama is weakening. As it was a long time ago, now the love for his own daughter is weakening him. He is experiencing the same turbulence as he had experienced two thousand years ago, when he was king Samudragupta rejected by a courtesan.

Now all over again he is doubtful and suspicious of Ram, doubtful of his own capacity, doubtful of his own existence, doubtful of his own purpose.

Ram is in love. His passion was interrupted thousands of years ago when he was Agustya. Now he wants it back. Now he not only wants back his Urvashi in the form of Natasha, he also wants all the power and all the glory that goes with that love.

Natasha also is torn apart between her father the High Lama and her husband Ram. She knows that she cannot trust her father, yet she loves him, and she also loves Ram. She feels that Ram is alive. She feels desperate. She decides to find Ram on her own.

Thinking that somebody must have seen or heard something about Ram, Natasha feverishly was trying to find a way to rescue her beloved. In her mind she saw heart chilling images of Ram, unconscious, helpless, yet alive, and carefully guarded by the silent wilderness of the Himalayas.

Amidst this fast unfolding drama, a feeling of hope suddenly entered Natasha's heart. This feeling came with a thought of Ram's Master and a strong urge to see him, as if the old mystic had something important to tell her.

This inner feeling intensified to the point that she could not wait nor think about anything else any longer, except the Master of Ram.

The energy of a peaceful grove, where the Master lived, entered her heart. And in her mind she saw a hazy valley. Natasha saw the Master's eyes looking at her with love and affection.

It felt as if she was watching an old movie, looking through a familiar blurry landscape that she could not remember. It felt as if she was lost and was trying to find her way to an unknown yet deeply desired destination.

For a split second she saw herself encircled by gigantic mountains. Feeling in awe in front of these colossal monuments of strength, she asked the mountains to keep her Ram safe and protect him from the scorpion sting of her father.

She didn't know why the High Lama, who had sent Ram on a mission of no return and planned to destroy him, was now desperately trying to find him. She didn't know what had changed in the High Lama's agenda. She did not know if she could ever trust her father or forgive him for what he had done to her and Ram, and make peace with her past.

She was trying to convince herself that something had changed in her father's agenda, and now he was ready

111

and willing to reconcile his convictions about Ram. Her heart melted. She suddenly felt how much she wanted to be with her papa at this moment, and how much she missed him; yet she was afraid to admit these feelings to herself.

For a moment she became the child she used to be. She felt her father's strong arms lifting her up, putting her on a high wooden stool, and proudly announcing that she is going to recite Pushkin's poetry for their guests.

"Oh, papa, if you just knew what is in my heart," she whispered. Feeling nostalgic and longing for a father's love, she reached for her wallet, opened it, and slowly pulled out her hidden treasure, an old black and white photograph of her father holding her on his lap when she was a little girl.

Weakened by loneliness and troubled thoughts, Natasha travelled through a distant past, until her mind got exhausted and her body became inflexible and heavy.

"What is the matter with me?" she thought, trying to stay awake. "This way I will exhaust myself before I even start my journey. I must concentrate all my efforts on finding Ram. I shall not feel anxious or fearful. I must stay composed. I must think success."

Fully clothed, she climbed on her bed and plunged into oblivion.

CHAPTER 12

THE
ENIGMA
OF A ROUND CAVE

A Prophetic Dream

Natasha dreamt. She was on a small mountain horse, carefully moving up a steep mountain, avoiding sharp stones, and watching every step along her way. Her horse was climbing higher and higher until the road ended. There was nothing in front of her, but a bare mountain range covered by glistening white snow.

And before Natasha noticed, her small brown mountain horse suddenly became a white Pegasus. It was effortlessly flying higher and higher, as if it knew exactly where it was going. Finally the Pegasus landed on a small plateau, surrounded by high mountain peaks.

Natasha saw a cave in front of her. She entered the cave. There was a figure in a white robe, sitting by a water stream running down from the belly of the mountain. The cave was round and tall. There were trees and flowers, growing around the stream. It was warm.

She thought she was in Paradise. She never felt as peaceful and lighthearted, as she felt at that moment.

"That figure in white must be Ram," she thought and called him:

"Ram, I am here. I came to take you home," she said, but Ram did not move. She could not see his face, yet she knew that it was Ram. She wanted to come closer and look at his face and touch him, but she couldn't.

"Ram, Ram, Ram," she called loudly, and woke herself up.

Natasha tried to resist waking. She wanted to go back to sleep and to see Ram's face, but she couldn't enter that world again.

Yet, she remembered her dream. She felt that it was a sign that Ram was alive, waiting for her help. All of a sudden everything had been decided.

"I am going to go; now, today. My Ram himself has come to me in my dream and showed me the way to find him. I am not telling anyone about my decision. I am going now… I will find him."

Natasha was talking to herself loudly as a mad person would do. There was no focus or trace of peace on her exhausted face. She was trying to control her temporary madness, caused by her anxious urge to help Ram this very moment, now, but did not know how.

With all her might Natasha was making an effort to push away the flow of negative thoughts that were bombarding her mind from all directions. Totally exhausted she stopped in the middle of the room and looked at her completely changed world.

In that moment, something had changed in her heart; something that she consciously practiced all her life, but had not mastered yet. It was something that she was teaching her students and envied in her father and Ram, a clear vision.

Her whole being had changed. She matured. She felt free. This new feeling was meaningful and worthwhile. It filled Natasha's heart with ecstasy and also with a bit of fear. This new feeling gave wings to her soul and brought a clear vision of union with Ram. She was expecting a miracle.

The only person Natasha thought of asking for help was Keith Andersen. Keith Andersen was the one who convinced Natasha that she must attend Ram's seminar. And she was grateful to him for that.

She knew very little about this man. Yet the way he expressed his personal admiration for Professor Roy made Natasha feel that he might know much more about Ram than he was expressing.

"Perhaps, he belonged to the same secret society as the High Lama and Ram," she thought. She wasn't sure if she could trust him. She wasn't sure if Keith Andersen was loyal to Ram.

And as always, when she felt uncertain or doubtful, Natasha asked the question and turned inward for guidance. She heard the voice. It was the voice of her Inner Teacher; a single gentle voice without flattery or judgment, without instruction or orders to follow. That voice brought a feeling of peace to her whole being. With complete reliance on her Inner Teacher, Natasha picked up the phone, and called Keith Andersen.

He answered. And, as she expected, immediately offered Natasha his help with no conditions attached. The next day the two of them were on the plane to Kathmandu.

Following her inner feelings, Natasha decided to take the same route as she had taken with Ram eight months earlier, when he brought her to India for the first time.

That trip had designed this moment. On that trip Ram did not tell her who he was. He prepared Natasha to realize that he was a man who plays many roles in his life and has many faces.

She did not question him then. She was in love. Love knows no reason and no limits. She just wanted him. All her reasoning faculties had vanished in front of Ram's magnetic brown eyes with the blue band around them. That night Ram asked her to be his woman and marry him with the moon, and the sky, and the stars as their witness.

She desired no other man, but Ram. She wanted Ram with all her heart. She longed to be Ram's woman that night and every night until the end of time.

Ram knew an old mystic who lived in that area in a small hut. He called him the Master. Ram told Natasha that at the Master's feet he found peace. He brought Natasha to his place and asked his Master to bless him and his bride to be; and to perform the wedding ceremony as it was done thousands of years ago.

The old mystic blessed them. And when the full moon took over the sky, and the constellations that are auspicious for a marriage had appeared, a sacred fire was lit, and Ram's Master began the mystical ceremony of marriage.

He took Natasha and Ram seven times around the fire. The light of the fire filled up their hearts with ecstasy and delight. They became one with the fire and light. The ultimate union took place. Two souls merged into one forever.

Kathmandu welcomed Natasha and Keith with a glorious sunny day. Blown by the wind from the mountains, Natasha's golden hair was flowing behind her, reflecting the glory of the sunrise. She felt excited. She felt Ram's presence. She felt that she was already in the arms of the man she loved; the man she had chosen, as an ultimate answer to all that had meaning in her life.

The snow capped mountain peaks looked exactly like those she had seen in her dream. Their shades and colors were strangely unusual and unknown to her senses. Cold and distant, they were not inviting her to come close, but almost ordering her to keep a distance and admire them from afar. It felt as if they were guarding deeply hidden secrets of life, desired by many, but only revealed to a special few.

A Nepalese soldier appeared. He was the same man who welcomed Natasha and Ram when they arrived in Kathmandu for the first time. He silently greeted Natasha and Keith, and, with a half hidden mysterious smile, made a sign to follow him. Without words everything was said and understood. There was no need to talk. Natasha and Keith knew that they had arrived into the High Lama's domain.

The little village was approaching. Natasha could see small cottages hidden behind the trees. The warm feeling of belonging to this land and to these gentle people enveloped Natasha's heart. Even though she was here only for a short visit with Ram, everything felt familiar, as if she had lived here for a long time before.

The soldier's wife Shanti welcomed Natasha and Keith to eat with them. Their humble place and simple food were therapeutic and nurturing for Natasha's body and soul. All of a sudden she felt at peace.

It seemed to Natasha that she was here just an hour ago; and now she came back to finish her meal. She forgot the eight longest months of her life, where each day was like a lifetime of waiting for Ram's return.

All her past, present and future had vanished in this moment. There was nothing but infinity, staring at her with its perplexing mysterious eyes, which had no feelings and no emotions.

The soldier's voice broke the long silence: "The High Lama wants to see you," the soldier said looking at Natasha. "His driver should be here any moment to take you to the lamasery."

Natasha nodded her head politely without saying a word. In her mind she went back in time. As if it was yesterday, she saw herself as a new bride just arrived at the same lamasery with Ram to meet his mentor, the High Lama.

Was it a meeting of fate, or was it a meeting predestined thousands of years ago? Or was it a meeting that each one of them had planned without realizing that they had planned it?

"Ah, what an enchanting play this life is!" she thought. "There must be something important that brings me back to this small village that seems so familiar. What could it be? Why am I here again? What is here that I must find, yet cannot see? How can I make myself to see it, and to make peace with my past; and to stop running away from my problems?"

She was an eighteen year old rebellious girl living in Russia, when she left her father's home and ran away to England to be free from the domineering ideology of her father that she did not want to accept.

After twenty years of separation from her father, Natasha unexpectedly met him here, in this remote place. She hardly recognized her father in his strange clothes.

Yet, it was him, her papa; the closest person to her in the whole world.

Yet, before the day of their reunion ended, she ran from him again. This time she found that her father, now the High Lama and Ram's mentor, wanted to destroy her Ram. She could not allow this to happen. With a broken heart Natasha left her beloved father for the second time.

"It seems history likes to repeat itself," she thought. "What am I running away from, every time I face the problem? What did I achieve by doing this?" She thought.

Suddenly she saw her life clearly, as if a strong wind blew away a heavy fog separating Natasha from herself. She suddenly realized the futility of her efforts to run away from her problems, because her problems were running along with her, and she was not able to shake them off. She saw the futility of her efforts to change the course of events. She was helpless in front of the law, the Law of Karma.

None of us can escape the iron grip of the Law of Karma. None of us can hide or run away from our problems, for our problems will come back with a vengeance and haunt us.

Now Natasha was ready and even eager to face her father; she was ready to resolve their differences and problems on a higher level of understanding.

The soldier's wife served the tea made out of thick yak's milk. The strong distinctive smell of this tea penetrated Natasha's nostrils, but did not bother her this time. Drinking slowly from a clay cup that the soldier's wife put in front of her, Natasha remembered to say 'mmm' after every sip, exactly as Ram taught her before.

While her body was relaxing in a humble warm hut and her facial expression was showing enjoyment from every sip of tea, her conscious awareness entered another dimension, another lifetime…

As on a big movie screen, Natasha saw her father dressed as a king and the young princess Sangita riding on their horses towards a small temple. There a princess, who was forbidden to dance all her life, put her first ankle bells on, and took her first dance steps.

She saw Sangita's dance. It was magical, as if the greatest experts of the world had trained her for a thousand years. She danced until she reached total exhaustion and fell unconscious at the feet of Shiva. She saw the king lifting her up from the floor and shouting out: "Urvashi, you have not left me!"

The sound of the king's voice pierced her heart and brought Natasha back to the small hut; but just for a moment, to have a sip of the tea, and to return back to the king, and to the princess, and to the old temple.

She heard the king's voice again telling the princess about her mother Urvashi. She heard the story of a gorgeous courtesan, her own story. It was a story of ultimate love, a story of perfect beauty, and perfect harmony.

It was about a gift of eternal youth from a sage to a courtesan; the gift that transformed a courtesan, who mastered the art of entertaining and courting men, to a courtesan of the heavens; a courtesan, who mastered the art of entertaining and courting the love of the universe.

She heard the king's confession, telling that he killed to love, but he was never loved... Suddenly the voice of the king weakened and disappeared in the loud sound of the car engine outside the hut.

Natasha came back from her trance, trying to remember where she was. The High Lama's driver just arrived and was waiting for Natasha and Keith to come out to take them to the lamasery.

It was time to say goodbye and leave this warm place to face the wind of another frontier; the destination, the vision that she had consciously chosen to feel all that she could feel.

The bright charming smile of a young Sherpa driver greeted her at the front door. He helped Natasha and Keith to get comfortable for a head spinning drive on the snaky road to the lamasery.

With every curve of the narrow road around the mountain, Natasha's emotions were escalating and intensifying the feelings of joy and fear. She knew that it would take a miracle to open her father's heart. She knew that it would cost her a great deal of patience to understand him; a man of the deepest contradictions and also of the deepest urge for the true love that he had never experienced.

It demanded the sacrifice of the mature woman that she had now become. This woman knew how to love.

The thing she needed most next to love was her freedom. Being free, being independent was not negotiable for her.

The snaky road to the lamasery was twisting and winding around the mountain. Yet it was not the same road she had been driven on the first time. Now it was the road that led to the heart of her papa. Excitedly she hurried on.

CHAPTER 13

THE
BAIT
OF LOVE

In the Web of Anguish and Joy

The High Lama waited for his beloved daughter in the sanctuary of the lamasery. His being was consumed with anguish and joy battling for position in his heart.

Anguish, because he was planning to make his daughter into a widow to protect her. He was planning to use her as bait to find and kill Ram.

Joy, because he was feeling that embrace of love, the pure serene love, which his heart was thirsting for so he could fulfill his mission of a father that was incomplete.

There was no joy in that joy. It was an empty feeling. Anguish took the stronger position. Each moment seemed an eternity in that waiting. He visioned the inevitable, the elimination of his Ram, who was closer to him than his own daughter. Yet in his mind Ram was the cause of all his anxiety.

Sitting in the sanctuary and contemplating his intention to annihilate Ram, he felt uncomfortable for the first time. It was mind numbing. He realized that Ram was his own reflection. Yet there was a difference.

The difference was that Ram had realized the futility of the Society's Mission and wanted to pursue a path of Individual growth and attainment.

And the High Lama was not prepared to accept that proposition yet. His life long quest would be in vain.

This was the vanity that was driving him insane. This insanity brought all his senses to a standstill. It felt as if his intellect had frozen.

The only hope he had was that Ram was dead. His idea of saving his daughter from Ram was just a justification for his own safety.

Anguish, vanity, fear, and a sense of purposelessness culminated into an intense hate for himself which his mind had transferred to Ram, his son, his own living reflection.

The High Lama was caught in the cyclone of a violent anger that was about to destroy his own house of cards that he had built around the renewed love of a father and a daughter. He hoped intensely that Ram was dead and that he did not have to go through with the plan of neutralizing Ram.

The High Lama heard a soft inner voice saying: "Not that I loved Caesar less, but that I loved Rome more," the justification of Brutus, the closest friend of Julius Caesar, when he assassinated Caesar. He found his reasons now.

The High Lama was awoken from his reverie by the sound of the jeep bumping its way through the graveled steep and winding road towards his cottage next to the Sanctuary.

His heart leapt with joy and he could not contain himself. He dispensed with the formalities of bowing out of the Sanctuary and ran and bowed before the beauty of his seed, and embraced her. The desire of love of a father met its culmination.

The embrace was eternal. In that embrace Natasha felt the strength of Ram and the comfort of total unconditional love. She became a child with the maturity of a great teacher. She was euphoric.

Natasha saw a blur around her and could only feel the warmth of her father's embrace. It was totally different than the embrace of Ram. It was joy transcending all other joys. And yet a father's love has no fulfillment in it. The fulfillment is in the husband. A husband's embrace is an adventure, a call to self destruction to become the butterfly from the chrysalis. The father's embrace is the comfort of the cocoon. This cocoon, the father, did not want this chrysalis to join in the glorious adventure of becoming the butterfly.

Natasha closed her eyes while still in that embrace, and in total trust, as she remembered from the past, said:

"Papa, I want my Ram and you. Can you give him back to me?" It was the great irony of the beckoning of love.

Tears started rolling down her cheeks and they moistened the cassock of the High Lama. The emotionally charged father now felt that he should be able to raise the dead to life, and must make Ram live again.

He somehow knew in spite of all indications to the contrary that Ram must be alive somewhere, lurking to get his beloved daughter back. The High Lama also knew that, if this was the case, then Ram has become more dangerous than ever before. He knew that.

He trained Ram. He saw Ram in action. The man that he trained was an emotional warrior; but to pursue his cause, he would transport himself into a cold, unfeeling man and have no compunction to destroy his own trainer, his own mentor, his own adopted father.

The High Lama smiled and heard a voice within saying to himself that he would do the same; that he has done it already. He designed the killing of Ram. Yet he could embrace his own beloved daughter with the emotion of the most affectionate father, while at the same time, he planned her husband's death.

The High Lama could justify all the atrocities that he had committed under the banner of the glory of mankind and of justice. He pondered:

"Whose justice?"

In the midst of this embrace a lifetime passed. The High Lama felt that he had experienced this pain before somewhere in eternity. The warm embrace that he was engulfed in became cold. He felt that the woman that he had loved somewhere in a different time, though in his embrace, could not give him a woman's love. She already gave her love to a man, who he desired to eliminate, because he was a threat to his emotional and temporal life.

The silence of the embrace was the eye of the storm that was raging in the mind of Natasha and her beloved father, the High Lama.

Natasha whispered gently in the right ear of the High Lama while resting her tender face on the right shoulder of her powerful father:

"I love you papa."

The world vanished for the High Lama. He had seen the world. He had changed governments. He had trained leaders and felt completely invincible; now he melted, became a father, the strongest human in the world... A Father loved by a Daughter.

Natasha said:

"I know papa that Ram is not dead. I know papa that he cannot be dead. I am his soul; and I feel him. It is not the madness of a wife, who is in love with her man."

The High Lama kept silent and watched her beauty. He remembered something that he could not explain to himself, let alone verbalize it.

The High Lama also had a feeling that Ram was not dead. He knew that Natasha would know, but now he realized that Natasha was not certain. He also knew Ram's capabilities; that he could not find Ram, if Ram decided not to be found.

He taught him to change the teacher's tactics like you must change your passwords now and then. Ram was taught by him not to trust anybody and not even the teacher. The teacher may be the assassin himself.

The High Lama knew his only means to reach Ram was through Natasha. He also knew that, if Ram was alive, his own life was under an imminent threat. He also knew that a man like Ram could not be a husband and love his daughter. He must eliminate Ram.

The High Lama invoked the law that he himself learnt as a young man and which he taught to Ram: "The end justifies the means." He had no moral or emotional barriers to make Natasha, his beloved daughter, the bait to hook Ram.

The High Lama did not know why Natasha had come to that region. He wanted to find out. He did not know that Natasha also wasn't sure, why she herself came to that part of the world.

She just felt it. She heard her inner teacher, her inner voice, telling her to come. She almost felt that she heard Ram calling to her.

Natasha saw Ram in her dreams in the Himalayan region. She could feel him in the mountains. When she saw the sunrise against the snow capped mountain peaks and saw the glory of life; she felt that her Ram was watching the same vision and, in that, they were romancing.

The High Lama wanted to know, and at any cost, whether Ram was dead or not. He decided to give all the information that Natasha wanted and then follow her through his operatives in this mountainous terrain to find out.

One thing that Natasha wanted to do before making any plans was to locate the Master of Ram. Intuitively she felt that the old mystic would be able to help her to find her beloved.

The same Sherpa boy, who had brought Natasha and Ram to the Master's hut for their wedding ceremony eight months ago, was driving her now towards a small village at the foothills of the Himalayan Mountains where the Master lived.

They arrived in the evening. It was dark. The Sherpa boy helped Natasha out of the jeep and showed her the way to the entrance door of the Master's hut.

He was familiar with the place. The Sherpa boy positioned himself on the bench outside the hut as instructed by the High Lama. He saw inside through a small window into the dimly illuminated hut, and watched every movement of Natasha.

The High Lama's instructions were precise and to the point:

"Watch every movement of Natasha and never take your eyes off her at any time."

CHAPTER 14

AT
THE MASTER'S
HUT

The Trail to Destiny

The Master looked affectionately at the young woman standing at his doorstep. It seemed that he was expecting her. He smiled, gently nodded his head, and said with a loving voice:

"Come in, my daughter."

He made a soft gesture with his right hand showing Natasha the straw mat on the floor in front of him, while he sat on the small bed in a yoga posture for meditation.

"Sit down, my daughter," he said quietly.

"Welcome to my home. I hope you will feel comfortable here."

His look was the epitome of serenity. It seemed that he was the source of the river of love of this Universe. His gentle smile made the hurricane lantern that was flickering in the dark unnecessary; as his smile lit up the world.

"I came to find my Ram, Master." Natasha said, reverently bowing her head before the old mystic. 'Can you help me?"

The Master closed his eyes, went into a trance, and entered Natasha's heart. He was not surprised to see how much Ram meant to this beautiful enchanting woman. How ecstatic, complete, and joyful Ram made Natasha's life. The Master saw how much Ram had affected her whole being by bringing a full new meaning into Natasha's existence. How he rejuvenated her heart and made her beauty blossom.

Yet there was a price. A high price she had to pay to receive these gifts. It was the hardest time of Natasha's life; and yet, the most beautiful. The god of Love was guiding her heart. She was indomitable. She was ready to face all obstacles, even death itself, just to be with her Ram.

While she was sitting on the straw mat and waiting for the Master's answer, her heart was filled with anguish and love. The silence seemed endless.

At that time she did not know that all these tests and trials were a necessity for her own growth and her own cleansing to meet her destiny; the union with her lover. Her tests and trials were opportunities to perfect her entire being; and perfection, as we all know, is a continuing and an everlasting process.

At that time she couldn't see through the masks of appearances. At that time she did not know that the difference between her father's and her own behavior was only in their expressions, but their inner nature was identical. They both wanted the same thing from life; love and acceptance. Yet both of them were blinded by their egos and couldn't see the truth.

She thought how easily deep love turns into deep hate by the anguish of the ego. And, as a result, all other feelings reverse themselves into the opposite, negative, and self destructive emotions.

At that time she did not know that her tests and trials were not the cruelty of karma, but the gifts, leading her step-by-step from fears of darkness into joys of light.

She was going through excruciating pain to grow in understanding; to realize that healing and wholeness are only possible through love; to know that there is nothing worthwhile, but love; and to grasp that only love can bring the ecstasy of life, the eternal orgasm, which is the origin of creation of the Universe. This is the eternal orgasm of Shiva and Shakti, as Ram had explained to her, when he told her the metaphor of 'Yoni and Lingam'.

135

As strong as Natasha was, or appeared to be, she was like a river that had just begun a journey on its way to the ocean. She was struggling to find her own path through the moonless night of her life.

She was close, yet seemed so far away. She needed a living Master, a guide to show her the light of her own soul.

And now her soul brought her to the Master's feet. She was sitting in front of the old mystic, the Master of Ram, without knowing that it was her destiny to come to the doorway of this little hut, the doorway to her own enlightenment.

Natasha's soul was yearning to reach out and merge with her soul mate. That feeling was always alive in Natasha's heart. It was constant. It was burning. It was pushing her forever forward. It became her ultimate purpose. And behind that purpose there was a living inspiring power that she could not explain. Yet she felt it. And she knew that she would pursue this purpose to its final accomplishment.

She did not have the Key to Liberation yet; but she was intuitively moving towards the blazing trail, which was leading to her destiny; the destination that she had chosen two thousand years ago.

Her deep intense urge to find the secret of life, the secret of eternal youth brought her to this moment, to this remote place, to the feet of the Master.

Without realizing what she was doing, Natasha bent down slowly and touched the Master's feet with her forehead, as if she would be taught for a long time by a wise sage from the forest.

A lightening flash went through Natasha's body, as if she was pierced by a sword made of a blazing light that was brighter than the light of the sun.

The old mystic opened his eyes and looked at the enchanting face of a young woman. He waited, giving Natasha time to overcome the shock that she had just experienced.

"My daughter," he said in a quiet voice, "the greatness of your love brought you here today."

His gentle baritone reverberated in Natasha's ears, while he continued:

"Your yearning for union with your lover is a yearning of every woman's life. It is the yearning to find the man from whom she was separated before she took birth in this incarnation.

That is why, in spite of insurmountable difficulties, you found the way to this door. You violated all the rules of living that relate to the world of the external. Your soul recognized Ram as your soul mate. And it will not rest until you will find Ram again.

Let me tell you a story, my daughter. It is an ancient fable of a love that predates life. To experience this love we take birth as humans and suffer a lot through this excruciatingly painful life.

Life, as we know it now, is not a pleasurable event, or, should I say, that existence is a burden. The reason we take birth is to experience this love."

The Master closed his eyes and paused for a moment, recollecting the story. Natasha waited silently. A sudden calmness overpowered her anxious mind and she let serenity take charge of it. She waited with the anticipation that this story may enlighten her and help her to reunite with Ram.

Every moment seemed a lifetime. Silence dominated the dimly lit room with the hurricane lantern flickering in the dark.

Natasha could hear her breath. She became oblivious to her needs and her existence. The atmosphere became surreal. In that moment she experienced eternity. In that instant she touched life and rose above existence.

She opened her eyes gently. Her serene gaze fell upon the magnificent face of the sage that sat before her. She heard his voice, saying:

"Love denies death. And Yama, the Lord of Death, bows before Love."

The Master continued with the same comforting and enigmatic monotone, looking straight at the face of the enchanting beauty:

"Once upon a time there was a gorgeous princess Savitri, the daughter of a powerful king. The fame of Savitri's beauty spread faraway throughout the land. One day she told her father that she would like to go out in the world and find a husband for herself.

The king agreed. And Savitri began her wandering throughout the country, searching for a prince of her choice.

One day she was walking through a dark forest. In that forest lived a blind king that lost his kingdom. He lived there with his wife and a son. His son was a handsome young prince who devoted his life to taking care of his parents. He chopped wood, sold it, and bought food for his parents.

As soon as Savitri saw the young prince she knew that her search came to an end. She fell in love. The young prince was called Satyavan. He was kind and generous. Yet he was doomed to die within a year after his marriage.

When Savitri's father found out about the curse of Satyavan, he asked his daughter to select somebody else. Savitri refused to marry anyone else, but Satyavan. The king reluctantly agreed.

Savitri and Satyavan lived happily in the small hut in the forest for a whole year. On the last day of the year, Savitri asked Satyavan to take her with him to the forest to gather wood."

The Master stopped for a moment to have a sip of water from a brass cup that was on the floor next to the bed that he was sitting on. Those few seconds felt like an hour for Natasha.

Clearing his throat, the Master continued:

"Holding their hands, Savitri and Satyavan walked through the enchanting forest. They plucked

139

flowers on their way, rolled in the soft green grass, laughed and romanced.

Suddenly Satyavan felt tired. He lay down his head on Savitri's lap and died. Savitri carried Satyavan's body on a raft through the river of life to the dark gloomy house of Yama, the Lord of Death.

Through the darkness Savitri saw a tall figure standing before her. It was Yama, the Lord of Death. Savitri bowed her head, greeted Yama, and respectfully asked:

"Oh Lord of Death, give me back the life of Satyavan; or take me too, along with my husband to the land of the dead."

Yama replied:

"Your time has not yet come. Go back to your home. I can give you any boon you want, except Satyavan's life."

And Savitri asked for the boon:

"Oh Lord of Death, give me strong sons," she said.

"You shall have a hundred strong sons, Savitri," Yama proclaimed as his boon.

"But how can I have sons without my husband?" Savitri asked, and pleaded:

"I beseech you, oh Lord of Death, give me back the life of Satyavan."

Yama was helpless. He was conquered by the power of Savitri's love. And The Lord of Death brought Satyavan's body back to life."

The Master paused and held his silence for a long moment, then said:

"My daughter, woman is the soul of man, she is Savitri. Man seeks the love of Savitri to regain his immortality."

He paused again, and then said:

"This is not an allegory, my daughter, this is your and Ram's story. You have played out this story from eternity to eternity. Dwell on this story, and you will find all the answers to life. You will find your Truth and your Immortality."

The ever soothing voice of the Master penetrated right into Natasha's heart bypassing the questioning intellect. She knew it was the truth. She knew it.

Natasha's eyes lit up.

"What shall I do, Master?" She asked eagerly, ready to go to the end of the world if it where necessary to bring back her Ram.

The Master lowered his voice so that only Natasha could hear him; he moved his body slightly forward towards Natasha and mysteriously whispered in her ear:

"Do not look for Ram anymore. You don't need to find him. Ram is in your heart. Go back. Go home, my daughter. Meditate. You will find the new power in you. Learn to use that power. With that power you will find yourself. And in finding yourself, you will find Ram."

The Master got up from his seat. For a moment he vanished in a far dark corner of his hut. Natasha heard the sound of water being poured in a small vessel. She heard confident steps of the old man approaching her.

"You must be thirsty," he said, putting in front of Natasha a shining brass cup filled to the brim with cold water.

"Our water is sweeter than the water in your big cities," he said with a child like smile, "try it, my daughter. I think you will like it."

Natasha had the first sip from the shiny brass cup and nodded.

"It is sweet," she said with her charming smile; "I never knew that water could be so tasty," she said.

Drinking slowly, she felt an unusual power, flowing through her body and calming down her excited senses. Natasha finished drinking, smiled happily, folded her hands, and said with gratitude and affection:

"I thank you, Master. I shall follow your guidance and do everything as you said."

She got up from the straw mat on the floor and moved towards the door. While leaving the small hut, Natasha reverently bowed to the Master again. Her heart was overflowing. She felt renewed.

Filled with an anticipation of union with her lover, Natasha rushed outside. All she desired at that moment was to go back home and prepare herself for the meeting with Ram.

The Sherpa boy was still outside, patiently waiting for Natasha to take her back to the lamasery as per instructions of the High Lama. In silence Natasha followed him to the road and got into the jeep. There was nothing that she could say to the young Sherpa boy or he could say to Natasha.

The small village vanished behind the moving Jeep, swallowed by a pitch dark cold night. But Natasha's heart was filled with light and with a warm affection for everything around her. She was a different woman. She was prepared to meet her destiny. She was Savitri, ready to reclaim the life of her Satyavan.

She was going back in total trust, in expectation of a miracle about to happen. She was ready to learn, to change, and to understand the change. Change as the origin of all things. Change as a thread that binds together life and death with a never-ending string. Change as an embrace, as a dance of the real and unreal. Change as Life Eternal.

CHAPTER 15

THE FLIGHT
THAT NEVER
ARRIVED

A Mystery

Hidden Behind a Plane Crash

While Ram was exploring the scenery flying over the mystical land of the Himalayan Mountains, the gold of the sun was spreading upwards like a gigantic net, until it covered the whole mountain range with its glorious splendor.

A stretched out horizon was sparkling against a far-away blue sky; and the mountains were changing colours from light blues at the top of their peaks, to darker blues, and almost black, towards the lower slopes.

Looking at the golden sunrays, spreading over the snow capped mountain tops, Ram was seeing Natasha's golden hair, shimmering on the white pillow in the hotel suite in Paris last night. He could still feel the sensation of Natasha's captivating fragrance on his jacket: a mixture of Miss Dior French perfume with wild flowers of a tropical forest.

In his mind he experienced union with his lover again; and felt the urge to express his feelings in poetry.

As Ram was about to reach for his notepad, his mood suddenly changed.

"What could it possibly be?" he asked himself, trying to understand, where his chilling thoughts were coming from. He looked through the window to see if he could recognize the location below.

He had been travelling over this route for a long time; and could clearly see that he was flying over Kanchenjunga, which is the world's third highest mountain peak, nestled in the Himalayas, close to Sikkim, the land of mystery and splendor.

At that very moment there was an explosion. Fear of death numbed Ram's senses. His private jet was attacked, but Ram did not know who the attacker was. He heard the pilot's voice shouting something, perhaps urging Ram to hold tight to his seat.

Through the window Ram could see sharp rocks quite close, yet fuzzy, because of the speeding down plane. In a few seconds the plane crashed in the wilderness of a mountain jungle. Ram was thrown from his seat and hammered next to the cockpit.

After being unconscious for a few minutes, Ram opened his eyes. He saw himself bruised and bleeding, laying next to the pilot, who was dead. As he watched the blood flowing from the pilot's chest, he thought that it was he, who died.

He saw himself moving through a long tunnel of light and heard a distant voice. It spoke to Ram and said:

"Rise, Ram Shankar Roy."

Ram thought that he was hallucinating, but the same voice repeated again:

"Rise, Ram Shankar Roy, and get out of the plane."

"I must be dreaming all this," went through Ram's mind. Yet, he made an attempt to get up and tried to push his body towards the exit. But it was heavy and did not move.

"I must do something," Ram thought, motivated to action by that mysterious voice, which was still ringing in his ears.

He stretched his shaking body and tried to get on his feet, but couldn't. Suddenly he felt himself being lifted up by a powerful force, moved towards the wide open exit door, and thrown from the plane.

And as soon as he had landed on a soft blanket of snow, the plane exploded and burned to ashes. Shivering from a freezing wind, Ram looked around and realized that he was alone in the wilderness; and he also knew that it would take a miracle to survive.

The landscape was beautiful and serene. There was not even a trace of habitat; just miles and miles of pristine wilderness. Oblivious to Ram's problems, the sun was still flirting away with mountain tops, as if nothing had happened; and the birds in ecstasy were greeting a glorious new day.

"Something good shall come out of this," Ram thought, surprised that this seeming disaster did not lower his spirit. He knew that it was not an accident, for there are no accidents in life.

"So there must be a good reason hidden behind this crash and my survival," Ram thought. He did not know yet, but subconsciously felt that his karma brought him to this place, because of what he had done, or undone in his past life. He was here, because he had a strong desire, which could be accomplished through this experience, by being here at this moment.

Understanding the nature of this seeming trouble, Ram was curious to find out the mystery hidden behind his dramatic arrival He made an enormous effort to lift up his heavy body from the blanket of snow on which he had landed, and slowly got up. His feet were still shaking.

He witnessed himself standing alone on a tiny plateau, bewildered, with his eyes wide open, repeating again and again:

"Something good shall come out of this."

And as if by magic his pains vanished and hurts faded away. Suddenly he realized that there were no more needs left in his life: no mission to accomplish, no wrong

148

things to right, and no enemies to conquer. The last enemy he had was looking now straight in Ram's face, a lingering fear of dying.

And, as always, in the moments of calamity he thought of his Master and asked for guidance.

A shimmering light appeared before Ram's eyes, and a voice spoke to Ram:

"To be here now is your destiny, my son, for you had desired it a long time ago. Do not doubt the circumstance. Your urge to return to your true state and glory brought you here.

You have completed all your learning. You have accomplished many great deeds. You have finished the unfinished kiss and gratified all your senses. Yet, you still hunger for one more thing, Ram Shankar Roy.

Now you are ready to learn, what you could not learn before, because your priorities were different then.

You are here to conquer your last enemy- death, and to ascend at will."

"Thank you, Master," said Ram, folding his hands, bowing, and reverently asking:

"Tell me, Master, what shall I do?"

And the Master said:

"There is a hot spring in the cave, below this terrain. Go. You shall find there all you need. Meditate from morning to night.

When your ears will be open, you will hear my voice guiding you to the door of the 'other side', where nothing dies and nothing is born…

Ram found the hot spring in a cave surrounded by a sanctuary. There was all that he needed to be nourished and healed; and all that he needed to strengthen his spirit, and to see the light of his soul.

He meditated from morning until night, day after day, after day… until the light inside him became a blaze. His ears opened; and he heard the voice of the Master:

"Truth is but One," he said. "But men call it by many names. Your journey is to find your own truth, my son. You have realized that there is more than a war between different leaders to rule the world. There is much more than that, my son, much more… There is eternal Peace, Life that never ends.

You are now at the door of understanding that there is no death. I shall guide you no more. The rest you will learn from contemplation of Life.

Listen to the breath of the wind; it is your own breath. Become the wind and free yourself from the prison of your body.

Always remember to hold a clear vision of what you want to become. Be victorious, Ram Shankar Roy."

The Master's voice mingled with silence, leaving Ram surrounded by a world of illusions. That world was composed of fragments of his own imagination, changing and evolving according to his thoughts and conscious awareness of the things that he had contemplated upon.

He contemplated on every breath and movement of the nature around him. Nothing was small or insignificant to him. He watched the sun opening its eyes at dawn, and contemplated its glorious triumphant movement over the mountain tops. He followed the sun's journey through the bottomless sky until the eyes of the sun closed in a short sleep behind the horizon.

Ram observed the sun. The sun did not think or debate if it would rise tomorrow or not. The sun did not concern itself if it will warm the earth for good and kind people, and withhold its light from the violent and godless creatures.

It was just moving along its lustrous groove fixed in the heavens, without asking for rest or for a break. Satisfied and contented, in its complete golden wholeness; it was gazing around without feelings, detached from peace and violence, stillness and turmoil.

Yet, as a part of cosmic order, where everything is intertwined in one harmonious whole, the sun was subtly controlling life, making birds, flowers, and people wake up or fall asleep, work or rest.

Ram observed the mysterious moon at night, brightening up the distant dark sky, and saw it at dawn, looking tired and pale after a sleepless night.

Ram observed the powerful wind that had many voices and moods. He heard the wind giggling and laughing as a child. He heard the wind carelessly whistling as a happy traveler. He heard the wind whispering in his ears, as a gentle lover. He heard the wind's anger and hostility, as if it was a horrible monster.

Mystified by the wind's limitless power, Ram felt a strong desire to enter its spirit and become one with its dominance. The words of the Master were continuously reminding him:

"Listen to the breath of the wind; it is your own breath. Become the wind; and free yourself from the prison of your body."

Anticipating the feelings of freedom and delight to move at will in any direction, Ram was trying to access and to align his breath with the breath of the wind; practicing being in all places at all times; seeing himself without limit and form.

Day after day Ram was under the spell of that unpredictable, intangible, and unseen power of the wind. Contemplating the indescribable and the invisible, he became what he had contemplated upon. He became the wind.

Now Ram was ready to reap what he had sown two thousand years ago. At that time he was known as a sage from the forest, known as the great Agustya, who had the secret of eternal youth.

But there was Urvashi, the most gorgeous courtesan living in the tide of time. She danced before him. She seduced Agustya to taste the forbidden love. And he bowed to love and forgot for a moment about his quest: to rule the heavens and not the earth.

His patient soul was kept hungry and thirsty, longing and craving for progress and advancement. As a seed, which is longing in the earth to become a blossom and a fruit, Agustya's soul was striving to unfold itself toward higher expressions. And now his head, heart, and mind were supporting his soul, eagerly working together to reach a destination designed by his karmic deeds.

Now there was nothing that Ram desired more or wanted more than to follow his quest. Although he had no idea of how he would get the power, he knew where he wanted to be, and why.

He strongly felt that his destiny was shaping itself on its own. He felt that the plane crash was required to get where he wanted to be. It was an opportunity to break free from his mission and the High Lama. It was simply a gift. And this gift was given purely, because he was prepared and ready to receive this gift.

This understanding was appealing and tantalizing; it kept Ram deeply happy. It was leading him into an unknown bliss, the bliss of uncertainty. These new feelings had nothing to do with the High Lama's mission, which he had thought for a long time to be his own mission as well.

The memories of the High Lama's world were still fresh in Ram's mind. They were saturated with the feeling of reverence as well as a tinge of anger. Ram's thoughts of the High Lama filled his senses with all that seemed highly inspirational, unselfish, and ideal.

Yet they were also futile, shady, and frightening. They were emotions relating to a temporary, competing, and dying world. Ram thought he wanted to better that world.

But today he was sure that he was no longer interested in perfecting that world, but in perfecting himself. He had developed his own meaning of life and love, and had released his attachment to it. There was no more need for the High Lama's approval and recognition.

Following the instructions given by the Master, Ram's body had altered and increased the vibration of every cell to the level of light. Every day Ram was perfecting his ability to travel with the wind, until he became the wind.

He lived for a long time in this dream-life of numberless harmonic sounds and colours until his karma was satisfied in that direction.

One morning, when Ram was sitting upon his isolated highland in the Himalayan Mountains, contemplating, as always, on his breath and aligning his breath with the breath of the wind, he found himself floating in the air.

He looked down and saw his body. For a moment he felt frightened. His fear brought him back to his body. Yet, he experienced magic, a moment of freedom, a moment of divine beauty and power. In gratitude, he fell on his knees and wept.

As he perfected his out of body experience, he felt an intense desire to pass on this knowledge to Natasha. His desire to see Natasha was so powerful, that he was able to transport his thoughts to her. And she was able to receive his messages and follow through.

But this was not enough for Ram. He used to do similar things before with the High Lama, who taught him the art of controlling not only his own thought process, but the thought process of other people, and even directing their actions from a distance.

In the meantime Ram felt the need for more practice. He felt drawn to longer and longer contemplations. Now he wanted to have the freedom to take his body with him by increasing or decreasing the vibrations. He wanted to transport his entire physical embodiment from lower to higher density; and back from higher density to lower.

Ram felt that he had rediscovered his soul and was prepared to pursue its calling. He knew the destination. Yet he could not reach it without paying his last karmic debt.

CHAPTER 16

THE
MIRAGE
OF FREEDOM

Living the Dream
Amidst Daily Chores

The joy of freedom like a mirage was alluring Ram. It pushed him to practice his new skills more and more. Soon he was able to raise his vibration into light and take his body with him. He practiced incessantly until he knew that he could ascend and descend at will. He felt as free as the wind, unseen, powerful, and with no limits...

Yet Ram did not intend to manifest his body in front of Natasha. He did not want to complicate her life more than it had been already complicated by the High Lama who was following every step she made.

Two years passed by. Still the High Lama had no evidence of Ram's existence or death. He couldn't rest. He was doing everything possible to find the place of the plane crash to confirm to himself what really happened to Ram. But all his efforts were in vain... It seemed that a power, stronger than the High Lama's power, sealed Ram's secret forever.

Yet, just by looking at Natasha, the High Lama could sense Ram's presence in her. She had changed. She became peaceful and care free. Her slender body seemed lighter and was glowing from the inside out. Even her relationship with the High Lama had improved to unconditional love and acceptance.

Her intense desire to unite with Ram made her master all her powers and concentrate them at a point, from which she could communicate her thoughts and feelings to Ram. Distance was inconsequential

Awake, sleeping, or dreaming she was repeating the words of the Master:

"Do not look for Ram anymore. You don't need to find him. Ram is in your heart. Go back. Go home, my daughter. Meditate. You will find a renewed power in you. Learn to use that power. With that power you will find yourself. And finding yourself, you will find Ram."

Repeating these words helped Natasha to keep on waiting and stay centered on her vision. But at times she was losing her balance, feeling frightened and lost. There was nobody around her that she could talk with or open up her heart to.

Even Modhu, her best friend from England, who lived now in Santa Monica California and really loved Natasha, could not understand why her beloved Russian princess had closed her heart. Intuitively Modhu felt that there was much more than Natasha was able to tell her at the present moment.

All she could do was to wait for the right time to arrive when Natasha will be ready to talk about her feelings. She felt that now Natasha needed to be alone. Finally Modhu stopped insisting on getting together, as they often did before.

It was a great challenge for Natasha to continue to live in the world of the external that she could not enjoy. That was the cause of her pain.

And now through this pain she was about to learn the greatest lesson of her life. She was about to learn how to live in two worlds at the same time. She was about to learn how to enjoy external pleasures of life and yet live in eternity.

After Natasha's recent journey to the Himalayan range and meeting Ram's Master, she came back a changed woman. Still her mind wanted proof that Ram was alive.

Natasha's mind preferred the definite and the solid shape of Ram. Her mind wanted to see her lover's image in flesh and blood. Her mind wanted something reliable, existing now, and not in the future, at some later time, in another dimension.

Natasha's mind was trying to keep control and stay in charge by asking the same question again and again:

"Do you believe that Ram is as real as you are?" And Natasha's heart would answer:

"Yes, I do. I believe that Ram is as real as I am real."

At first she thought that she was dreaming Ram, but slowly she was able to convince herself that Ram was real. And Ram became real.

What was considered the real world for Ram became Natasha's dream world. She lived in her dream world more than in her real one. She was happy. Yet she was careful in expressing her feelings of happiness, because the ears of the High Lama were listening from every corner; and there was no place to hide.

Invisible for everyone, including Natasha, Ram was living and breathing next to her, reciting poetry in Natasha's ears, giving her long discourses, and challenging her mind to the point of complete exhaustion.

Ram loved his Natasha, his woman, his soul. He was transmitting to Natasha his entire knowledge; all that he had learned and practiced during all his lifetimes. He was pouring his awareness and his energy into her soul, which was like a cup that could never overflow.

She felt his energy, his every breath, every word, and every feeling that he aroused in her receptive soul.

And, as the Master had promised to Natasha, after assiduous practice of meditation, the miracle had happened: Natasha saw her own soul face-to-face.

And in the mean time, a spiraling fire within her being was slowly burning to cinders the old dross of limitations. And the same fire that was destroying the old structure of her body was building a new body for her, which was essential to the fulfillment of her vision.

This vision was as real for Natasha as her own existence. It was a vision of an ageless romance without beginning or ending; unbroken and, at the same time, it was as fresh as the morning dew.

It could never be satisfied or fulfilled. It was like an unfinished kiss with its unquenching thirst for more kisses. It was an ecstasy of union of two souls, where one soul is incomplete without the other.

It was mad, intense and passionate love that knows no restrictions or borders. It was the love that everyone yearns for and only few have known the rapture. When this union comes, then the body ceases to exist.

Natasha's friends and associates heard that she had married Professor Roy. Yet nobody ever saw them together. People wondered how this beautiful woman lived. She was always alone. Yet happy, smiling, and, they had to admit, that she was quite contented.

She was the subject of many conversations behind her back. Desired by men, and envied by women, she was leaving behind her a trail of mystery, as she passed by; an invisible trail of mystery and wonder.

But Natasha was not concerned. And if someone who knew her well would get the courage to stop her and ask:

"Where is your husband? You must really miss him. Don't you feel lonely?"

She would smile softly and then answer:

"No, I don't miss my husband. And I don't feel lonely." Then, instead of feeling displeased or annoyed by people's rudeness, she would kindly add with her usual charming smile :

"Don't you see? He is in my heart. How can I miss him? He is always with me."

Then, she would nod politely and move on, leaving people standing mystified, shaking their heads in disapproval, guessing and wondering what this mysterious professor could be doing, and why he was always away.

With time, the goddess in her made Natasha immune to such comments. Yet she was also a woman. And as a woman, she was not able to protect herself from the toxic venom of people's words which often left an invisible mark on her soul.

Then, the goddess in her would take over and refresh in her mind, the moments when she met Ram for the first time, their first kiss, his strong arms lifting her up and swinging her around.

And she would forget about the world, and the people, and the seeming troubles. Everything would magically change around her, filling her soul with Ram's mighty presence.

For a while she was not able to speak. She was able to hear only one loud heart beat. She would drown in Ram's eyes, trying to reach their bottomless depths.

In her mind, she would see the face that she loved so much, the face of a warrior and a lover; and she would whisper:

"I love you Ram. You are powerful and yet very gentle. I feel that I have known you all my life. Perhaps, this feeling comes from our previous lives together."

But in this incarnation for both of them it was their first love. The intensity and the longing were there from the very beginning. Every moment was an eternity, a declaration of perpetual joy.

Every night Ram's vital energy was poured into her being; and then his feelings expressed in a form of poetical compositions that were signed 'the Skywriter' and left on Natasha's desk.

Ram's poetry was Natasha's sustenance and strength. It uplifted her spirit and brought laughter to her heart. She was living in a world created by Ram's words, conjuring images of delight, laughing and giggling; even having long mental discussions with Ram, unknown to the outside world.

During their morning walks when people could see only Natasha, they were communicating to each other their deepest feelings and thoughts.

Who would know or even guess, looking at Natasha walking all alone with a mysterious inward smile on her face, that she was not alone at all.

She was walking along the lake with her companion, the poet and the lover, the transformer of her life. She was walking with her hero, the man who would not settle for glimpses of joy; the one, who taught her by his own example that love, conquers death.

Natasha was Ram's charm, a perfect creation of his imaginative universe. She was Ram's poetry, the epitome of womanhood and romance.

"I want to be always with you Ram," Natasha whispered in the cold morning air.

Ram answered:

"I will teach you how to enter into a state of unity with no beginning and no ending. It is my goal and my intention Natasha. You are my eternity. I shall take you with me to the land of perpetual bliss.

You were always with me. You had many names and many faces. I was reborn to give you what you had asked of me two thousand years ago. At that time I was a sage to be a king. And you were an enchantress, a gorgeous courtesan from the heavens. You came to seduce me and steal from me the secret of eternal youth.

At that time I couldn't give you what I didn't have. Two thousand years ago, I did not attain the union with the Absolute. I was almost there. But you had come and danced for me. Consumed by forbidden love, I lost my vision and bowed to your beauty.

Now we both came back to pay our karmic debts, and to realize our dreams. We are both here to purgate our desires, and to finish the unfinished kiss.

Now I am ready to fulfill my promise and to give you the gift you had asked of me two thousand years ago, the gift of eternal youth.

We will roam the universe together in perpetual rapture, in constant union of never ending orgasm. I will teach you and give you the secret."

Natasha loved to learn. She tirelessly practiced what she had learned from Ram. With time she was able to change her vibration to a higher speed and to travel in thought. Yet she was not able to raise her vibrations into light.

Her desire was to take her entire embodiment and to be able to ascend and descend at will, as Ram could.

She felt a sense of exultation of unlimited possibilities. She was anticipating the delight of freedom. She felt confident in becoming one with her lover forever.

Natasha dreamt it. She lived her dream amidst her daily chores. That was all that her thought could hold; and nothing else.

In her dreams she saw herself moving through continents, across oceans, and mountains, invisible and untouchable, one with her Ram; and one with the pulsating power of the universe that has no form.

She could only do it in her dreams. And it was as natural to her as walking and breathing. In her dreams she was able to get out of the density of flesh and dissolve into the fluidity of thought, away from the illusion of Maya.

CHAPTER 17

CONFESSION

The Last

Effort

Of a Masterful Ego

The High Lama kept vigil all night in the Master's hut. His thoughts were intense but focused on fear, instead of what he wanted to achieve. He, the High Lama, wanted love. He had never experienced the love that he sought and never got from Urvashi when he was Samudragupta.

He commanded love as he commanded his soldiers and got their obedience, but never got love. He never understood that love cannot be legislated, coerced, or commanded.

Love is the breath of life. Without love living becomes excruciatingly agonizing. A soul starved of love has no way out from the hell of life. Salvation is the tenderness of a lover's touch, a gentle smile before the embrace, and a life of total abandonment to caution. Love is devoid of fear.

Dawn was approaching with undue haste. The High Lama saw the dawn bowing before the Master's feet. And, as the High Lama expected, the Master arrived before dawn. He found the High Lama waiting for him in his hut.

"You look familiar," the Master said, looking at the High Lama with a smile that engulfed his soul.

"I remember you came here once. It was a long time back, perhaps more than twenty years ago. I cannot recall your name."

"I came from the lamasery not far from this place. They call me the High Lama there," the High Lama answered.

"Come, follow me my son," said the Master, moving towards the front door and leading him into the cold morning. "Let's sit outside and watch the sunrise together."

The High Lama followed the Master to a long wooden bench that the Master had made by himself from the trunk of a tree. He sat on a straw mat spread over the soft grass in front of the bench.

The Master sat on his meditation pillow on the bench and wrapped himself in a warm shawl. He looked at the High Lama, humbly sitting at his feet. Then, slowly nodding his head, the Master said with a childlike smile :

"You bring me memories of the illusory life that we do take so seriously. And yet we know that it is a frivolity that we want to enjoy, as we had enjoyed a game of hide and seek when we were little children."

The Master looked with his penetrating eyes straight through the iris of the High Lama and said without any connection to what he was just talking about:

"I was waiting for you to come. We both know everything about each other, my son. You are here, because you want to confirm to yourself that an action, which you are about to take, is not guided by your ego, but by the higher purpose that you follow.

You want to find the man that you had trained to serve you, and to become like you. And now you find him too dangerous for your own safety."

The Master started to laugh. And then he went into gales of laughter. He could not hold himself and said to the High Lama:

"I know that you had come to me before, but it was for a different reason. Do you really believe that you can manipulate the Universe to accomplish your end? Your philosophy, as far as I can say, is that the end justifies the means. Is that right?"

The High Lama felt a queasy feeling. He could not fathom where the Master was going. He graciously bowed before the Master and agreed, saying politely:

"Yes, I have dedicated all of my life to the welfare of humanity. I have practiced self control and performed my duties to the best of my ability. Yes, I have done everything in my power to help the world.

More than that, Master, I had become so obsessed with my duties to service humanity that my personal life ceased to exist."

"I understand you, my son," said the old mystic quietly, nodding his head.

"I understand you well. Every act of self-denial takes man a step forward towards perfection. And self-denial is the most important of all man's endeavors."

"Then, there should be no pain and no torments in my life. Is that right? Can you clarify this for me, Master?" The High Lama asked with humility.

"You, my son, know well how Nature works. Even this moment was planned according to Nature's secret chart and divine design. Nature is the embodiment of Karma.

Karma is binding. The Karmic Law is the very foundation of the Universe we live in. There is no escape from its iron grip other than transcending it.

When you drop a pebble in the vast ocean, the pebble drops to the bottom of the ocean, but that's not all.

The ripple created by the pebble reaches the edge of all the shores of the ocean. And after the ripple hits the edge, it returns back to the center.

The ripples don't ever stop flowing back and forth. Every action is like placing a pebble in the Cosmic Ocean. This is being caught in the iron grip of Karma."

Then, looking into the eyes of the High Lama with laser like rays, the Master continued in his gentle voice:

"You cannot undo what has been done, my son. You cannot stop the ripples of the ocean created by your actions."

"How can I then make amends and rectify what I did?" The High Lama asked in a slightly trembling voice.

"How can I make peace with myself, if I am unable to make my daughter happy? Am I to sit and do nothing and watch my heart, my daughter, being tormented because of my ineptitude? What must I do?"

The High Lama paused in a mode of surrender and the pause stayed unbroken and became silence that expected revelation.

The Master watched the High Lama ever so carefully as the rising sun was streaking gold on his serene face. The pause was for a moment, but it seemed like eternity for the High Lama.

Then the Master spoke in his authoritative voice. He said:

"You, my son, were trying to perfect the work of an artist, because you feel that the artist did not finish his art. You want to replace his work with your own distorted version of what his work should be.

Do you think that you are more merciful than the Universe or God, whatever you want to call this Power? Do you feel superior to that Omnipotent Power and form organizations to correct His mistakes? And in the process you appear to satisfy your ego and become a hero to a few and villain to many.

We have come into this world for us and not for anybody else. This may not seem as a noble idea to you, because you have given up everything. And now you think that you can pursue your quest for changing the world to protecting the world.

As great as it may sound, my son, don't you think it is an infantile approach to life? The genius that created you, this tree, the billions of stars out there, don't you think it knows what it is doing?

You are in essence like a little kid, trying to tell this infinite power that it is unfair and doesn't have the heart to love.

My son, the Universe has its own discipline. It is called the discipline of Karma. Pain, which you want to eradicate, could be the cure.

You don't even know why you pursue this path. It is because inside you dwells a masterful ego, which is self righteous, which wants to correct the mistakes of the Universe. Doesn't it sound ridiculous to you?"

The High Lama's ego felt hurt. He could not figure out where the Master was going. He took a deep breath, politely bowed before the Master again, and said bluntly:

"I confess. I had come with a mission to use you. I want to find out what can I do to love my daughter. And I also want to know how to avoid a confrontation and not to become a target of an assassination attempt by the man you and I know. That man is the only person that can destroy me, and he is your disciple. You are the Master; and you have made him invincible."

Dawn touched the feet of the Master. The dove's call for its mate agonized the yearning of nature to go into ecstasy of love. The mating call of the wild subdued the human yearning for fleeting pleasures of union.

The Master smiled again and said:

"You don't know what you want, my son. You only know one thing, and that is self preservation. That is what most people of this planet care about... Self preservation... You have used your own daughter for your own self preservation. Do you feel a sense of inadequacy?" the Master asked, paused, and continued,

"You don't need any preservation. You are immortal And the most pathetic part is that you know it. Yet, you don't believe that you are immortal You were never born and you will never die."

The Master continued with a childlike smile and said:

"Can you think of a time that you never were; and can you think of a time that you will cease to be?"

He started to laugh the childlike laugh that the High Lama was not very familiar with. The High Lama felt a bit deprived of life and laughter in the presence of the Master. He felt inadequate. He felt that he had missed out on some major paragraphs of his life in the process of living.

Then with a solemn voice the High Lama said:

"I have come to you for that very reason, the reason of love. And yet it all will sound so unreasonable. More than that, it will sound ridiculous and embarrassing."

The High Lama could not hold himself anymore. He was ready to confess to the old mystic and tell him all that he had carried in his heart for thousands of years. He was ready to open his wounded soul and reveal to the Master, what he was afraid to expose even to himself.

CHAPTER 18

THE PATH
OF
RETURN

Appointment With Destiny

The sun rose behind the mountains, playing the hide and seek game with the illusion of reality. The laughter of the wind was gushing fresh breath into a daydream of the Universe. This game was beyond the comprehension of the mind and the intellect.

The intellect did not dare to question the authenticity of reality, as if it knew that all existence is an illusion, as a solid dream is. And yet the dreamer does not want to awake from the dream. The dreamer and the dream are real in an unreal world.

The High Lama could not understand this new feeling of pain that was slowly growing inside his heart, until it ripened into a deep torturous wound and made him bitter and angry. He thought about his life filled with danger and sacrifices.

"Was it all in vain?" The High Lama thought, looking at the kind face of the Master, and then asked him aloud:

"What shall I do? How can I get out of the quicksand of life that I have set foot on? I want to be lifted up and be elevated to live a life that befits a man who wants to see no pain in this world."

"I understand you, my son," the Master said. "But the real reason you have come to me is to know how you can find Ram. You don't know if he is alive or dead.

In your business you cannot leave your enemy at large. You need to know where your enemy is at all times. You need to know the strengths and weaknesses of your enemy without fail. Without this knowledge you make yourself vulnerable."

"I know that you will not believe me," the High Lama answered, "but Ram is not my enemy. He is my son. And now he is my beloved daughter's husband. I do not have any desire to harm Ram."

"You cannot harm Ram anymore," the Master said with a mysterious smile, then paused, looking at the High Lama, who held his breath, waiting for the Master to continue.

"Finally I am going to find out what I was looking for," the High Lama thought. "All I want to know is if Ram is alive or dead."

And at the same time the Master said:

"He lives, but you cannot go where Ram is. He lives in a dimension that you must be prepared to travel to. And when you reach that dimension, you will realize that there is no death, no injury, and no hurt."

There was another long pause. The High Lama waited. The Master continued:

"In that world where Ram is you don't need a physical body, but only a subtle body.

Your physical body is the gross coating of the same stuff that your subtle body is made of, but at a lower vibration.

To reach that dimension where Ram is, all you have to do is develop the capacity to increase the vibration of your gross body to that of your subtle body. You are familiar with this theory. You can teach your students how to ascend and descend at will, but you cannot do what Ram has done.

What Ram has achieved is possible through the agency of a 'Master of Life'. The 'Master of Life' is the one who has the capacity to live in all dimensions."

Then the Master laughed an affectionate laugh and asked the High Lama:

"Do you want to see that dimension? Do you want to see, why you have come to me, and why you are so tormented? Do you want to see your son and your enemy, and to be at peace?"

"Oh yes, I do," the High Lama answered quickly and humbly bowed his head before the old mystic.

All of a sudden the Master touched the forehead of the High Lama between his eye brows. And the High Lama lost consciousness of this gross world.

He awoke in a different vibratory level, but the environment there was the same. He saw the same Master still laughing; and he was still sitting in the same place, where he had lost his consciousness.

He heard the voice of the Master saying gently:

"You are the same, my son, but the world where you had lived before cannot see you. Yet you can see them. Their eyes cannot catch this vibration. Just like in your previous world you could not see the ultra violet rays, and you could not hear sounds beyond certain decibels.

The same is here. This world has no death. What you called death in the world you came from is only a change of vibrations."

The Master's voice faded into silence. The High Lama went into a deeper trance. He saw himself spiraling down a blue iridescent bottomless hole. He did not feel any fear or concern of the outcome of this journey. He felt a sense of surrender, a sense of total trust and comfort. It was an enchanting surrender as opposed to a submission.

This feeling was enough for the High Lama to experience what a secure existence means. He felt protected in the midst of total uncertainty. He felt that he entered a zone of life, where there is no pain or pleasure. He, for the first time, felt bliss.

He could vaguely remember this bliss, when he had picked up Natasha from her mother's arms for the first time. He lost all worries and concerns of the future. He felt love.

In that trance all his memory of this existence faded in an instant; and he found himself in a different time and in a different land. A time far, far different than any he could imagine.

He saw himself clad in armor. He was returning from a battle with his soldiers. He was in Sarnath, where not long ago the great Gotama Buddha gave his teachings that would reverberate in the hearts of humanity for centuries to come.

Then he saw himself in a different setting. He was in a little village not far from Sarnath. He was standing before a woman, who had just given birth to a beautiful girl; the woman was dying.

This woman was his life, his love; and for whom he would lay down his crown and surrender his being to. He had lost her. He had lost her when he had thought that this beautiful courtesan could be commanded to love him.

She was Urvashi, the epitome of beauty; Urvashi, the trained courtesan, the desire of the gods. She was the enchantress of the heart and the body. Hell would be a cheap price for her love and her embrace.

Urvashi, the courtesan, was also the lover of Agustya, the king's brother. Agustya had abandoned the kingdom in search for the Truth of existence.

The sage Agustya was one step away from attaining the nectar of eternal youth, when the courtesan Urvashi found the sage in search of eternal youth. All three of them, the king, the sage, and the courtesan were obsessed with their desires and engrossed in their ambition. Aching and suffering, they were chained by their own karmic debts.

Now the great emperor Samudragupta was in front of Urvashi. She was speaking to him in a faint voice. She was saying:

"This is my daughter Sangita. Give her all the love that you would give to me. She is your daughter now."

Then she paused, gasping for breath. She was lying in the bed of a peasant, who had given her shelter in his little hut in the forest.

She realized that she had failed to experience motherhood and womanhood. She wanted both so intensely that she lost balance. She wanted both so deeply that she became immersed in fear. She was afraid of not getting it. So it happened.

Urvashi was dying. She clutched her beloved daughter for a few hours against her breasts. She said in a weak, but an enchanting voice to the man that loved her, yet could not get her with all his glory and power:

"She is the sage's seed. She is the daughter of sage Agustya, whom you murdered to get my love; and whom I deceived to get the elixir of life. We both lost."

Urvashi paused to take another breath and continued:

"I shall surely come back. Our love has to be completed before we can become deathless. I shall come to you as your daughter; and you will love me with all your life beyond the need for ownership. I will find Agustya and give him my love without wanting anything in return. I will love him."

She was exhausted. She wanted a sip of water. The peasant knew that the asking for the water is the last rite before the soul starts on its journey back home.

She lifted her head up with her own strength and took a sip from a brass cup. Then she continued in a fainter voice and said to the High Lama, who saw himself as the great emperor Samudragupta:

"I cannot ever take away the hostility between you and Agustya. You are, and will always be close but so far apart... When only both your egos are brought before the Master, then you can see the love that you always had for each other.

The paradox is that both of you are the same. You both are the paradox of life's relationship. I will come back to love both of you."

She took Sangita from her breasts and gave her to king Samudragupta, who was still in a state of trance, and said:

"Here is your daughter in my form. Love her."

She became motionless. Her eyes kept on staring at the powerful face of the emperor. The emperor gently closed her eyes.

Still in trance, the High Lama felt an agonizing pain in his heart. His courage to love leaped with jubilation, when he looked at the face of Sangita. He whispered to her:

"You shall never dance. You shall make the world dance for you, my daughter."

In that trance of total surrender the High Lama suddenly realized that he was not looking at the face of Sangita; but he was looking at the face of Roma, the daughter of Ram.

Roma's eyes, identical to the eyes of Ram, were deep and still, as a mountain lake. Her look penetrated the High Lama's heart. He knew what Roma was waiting for. She was waiting for the letter, which Ram had left for her in case of Ram's death.

The High Lama wanted to give her Ram's letter, but the image of Roma faded into emptiness. And from that emptiness Natasha's face emerged and flashed before the High Lama's eyes.

Silently he was watching an endless flow of images and sounds passing before his eyes. They were echoes of his personal yearnings for a tender touch of love.

"What have I done?" The High Lama thought, questioning his greatness for the first time.

"What kind of a man and a father am I? How can I expect a different life for me and my daughter, than the life that I had planned for Ram and his daughter?

Isn't it strange, how precisely I got back what I had given?"

The High Lama felt a sense of guilt and a sense of pain. He had used Roma, this beautiful little girl, to manipulate her father, Ram; Ram that he loved so much, enough to give him all the knowledge that he had.

Roma had kept Ram a captive to the High Lama. In essence, Ram knew that without the High Lama and without Ram, this daughter of his would be swept away by the tsunami of the enemies of Ram and by the daily mundane existence of this world.

Roma did not know who the High Lama was. She only knew that she had this mysterious guardian. She had a special number to call, when her father was not accessible, and leave a message.

Then a man with the most affectionate voice would call back and fulfill all her desires. She never saw him. She had often asked her father about this mysterious man and never seemed to have got a clear answer.

She did not pursue. She was trained not to ask when answers were not coming forth. She was told that it was for her protection. She knew better not to ask.

She was well protected; and yet she felt helpless. She knew that her father loved her; and yet she could not find the closeness. She knew that her father was a giant; and yet she knew that she did not know her father.

"How many boys and girls will never know their fathers because of me?" The High Lama thought.

He suddenly heard a familiar voice. That voice seemed to be coming from far away:

"Everything that was not fulfilled, comes back," said the voice.

The High Lama felt surreal in that trance. The sound of the voice brought a sense of peace that he never experienced before. He realized that he had lost the sense of time and space. He realized that all anxiety and all tension come from time and space, from the unforgiving past and the fearful future.

The dimension of time and space had been the High Lama's home all this time. He had lived in the world, where attachment was survival and loyalty had to be coerced or bought. He knew that the currency of the purchase of loyalty depended on the mindset of the person that was selling the loyalty.

He was the High Lama, the mentor of Ram. He knew what currency will work to buy Ram's loyalty. It was an emotional currency, and not the currency of power, or the hard currency of bank notes.

The High Lama heard the same voice again. And, in a distance, he saw a familiar form approaching. There was no fear or agitation, or sense of anguish, or excitement in seeing someone that he was looking for all this time. He said:

"Ram."

The High Lama opened his arms. He embraced Ram. And for the first time he felt that he did not have to buy the smile of Ram. For the first time he felt what a son is.

Ram did not say a word. And yet, they had a complete dialogue. Ram, without a sound, conveyed to the High Lama the love that he never knew and yet wanted.

"How strange," the High Lama thought. "How could I want something of which I had no knowledge?"

Then he realized that all knowledge is in him. He taught this to Ram before. But he was giving the theory of love, the theory that is trapped in time and space. But now he felt what love is.

"Ram, Ram, Ram," the High Lama could not stop repeating Ram's name.

"My son, if I were to die now, I would die the happiest man that ever lived. I came to find and play my destiny, the destiny of which I had no idea."

Ram made a sign of interruption by lifting the palm of his right hand towards the High Lama and said:

"There is no death here. I know what you are trying to tell me. I would not be here with you, if it was not for you.

You thought that I was the predator and you were the prey. And I thought that you were the predator and I was the prey.

We just could not reconcile our pains of the time when you took my Kingdom and I took your woman.

I am here to reconcile my relationship with you, my brother, my mentor, and my father. From this moment you are free."

The High Lama was calmly looking at Ram. The agonizing labor pain of his soul ended in a birth of tender love. And the seed of this tender love was planted in the rich soil of his liberated soul. He felt peaceful and complete.

"I am returning back," said Ram. "I shall see you again." Ram's form faded away, as if he was never there.

There was a long silence. Peace embraced the valley when the High Lama opened his eyes. He witnessed himself sitting on the same spot in front of the Master. He witnessed the Master's serene eyes and his gentle smile. He heard his voice saying softly:

"You should go back, my son, but before you go, I will tell you a little story."

'There was a young sage, sitting on the bank of the river Ganges and meditating. And his Master was sitting next to him.

On the river a little boat was struggling to raise its sails so it could catch the wind. The boatman was exhausted. Trying again and again, he gave up and sat down.

The young sage saw the difficulty of the boatman and with his new found powers raised the sail to help the boatman.

At the same time a horrific storm was blowing past and it caught the raised sail of the boat and capsized the boat. The boatman drowned and the boat sank.

The Master of the young sage admonished him and said:

"Do not interfere with other people's lives with your little new found powers. Just attain your own salvation."'

The High Lama sat quietly before the Master. They did not speak to each other for over an hour. Each of them was in their own worlds, journeying through the maze of the opaque world.

Finally the High Lama broke the silence and bowed before the Master. He touched the Master's feet and said with a sincere gratitude in his voice:

"Master, I feel I just woke up from a sleep. I must go and repair myself, and all I have done and undone. I will carry this story with me as a declaration of dissolution of this so called New World Order."

The Master blessed him and said:

"Today I ordain you as the High Lama. You don't have to hide behind the old mask of a High Lama anymore. You will find truth in your heart. You will find peace; and your presence will be peace.

Seek and you shall find your immortality. You will discover your divinity; and you will remember that this day was also the design of Karma."

A cold wind rushed from the North. It was blowing stronger and stronger, but the High Lama did not feel the cold. He opened himself up and let the wind take away all that was ingrained in him since his youth, since he joined the secret society.

For a moment he felt a sense of freedom. He felt the lightness in his heart, as if he would reach a climax of a peaceful relief or experience death.

Chased by the wind, the dark cloud that was hanging over his head as a guillotine for two thousand years, passed away. The High Lama's old self vanished. And a delightful expectation of liberty entered his heart. Serenity and peace saturated the air, dancing towards the horizon.

Soaked in a surreal world of mystery, the High Lama kept silent. While his body was sitting on the straw mat in front of the Master of Ram, he was experiencing oneness with the whole universe.

He knew that this moment was designed for reconciling his deepest contradictions; or at least for having a glimpse of peace that he was born to find.

He knew that this moment was a promise of a new life, where living was the source of eternal bliss.

He also knew that this moment demanded a great deal of sacrifice from him; his life's quest and his ideology.

Since his youth, he had renounced his personal life for his mission. He was never free to think and to do anything outside of his mission.

His cause required many sacrifices. And he had sacrificed all that he loved, and all that he cared for. He sacrificed his life and his personal freedom for the freedom of the world.

He was convinced that he was the missionary of freedom. And he continued sacrificing himself with pride, choking himself by drinking his own tears and getting intoxicated.

Constantly living in a world of hazards, being on guard every moment, he did not notice when his life became slavery and seemed unbearable. Following his path, and having plenty to do, he continued living this life of misery with clenched fists.

It took eternity for the hour of this morning to come. There was nothing he wanted more at this moment, or needed more than to know the truth; and to know how to complete this cycle of endless birth and death.

He simply wanted to know: who he really was; why he lived; and what the reason for his return was.

Suddenly he realized that he did not need to prove anything to anyone anymore, or to compete with anyone or any circumstances anymore, or even to create a better world for humanity anymore. He realized that he did not need to feel terrified by his thoughts or question himself anymore.

All he desired was to find himself, be himself, and be happy.

He felt as if he had come back to life after an attack of amnesia, a loss of memory for a long time, and tried to remember the reason of his return.

The High Lama touched the feet of the Master and left. The Master knew where he was going. The High Lama knew what he was seeking. He felt the thrill of life for the first time and lost the fear of death.

He became a mystery to the world. Nobody saw him again.

CHAPTER 19

EPILOGUE

A Secret of Eternal Life

In the realm of the mind
One can lose time and space

And enter eternity,
And live in the everlasting Now.

What is space?
And what is time?

It is but our imagination
Upheld by our intellect.

I like time, and I like space.
Isn't it what we are all chasing?

More time and more space?

In that time and space
We are also looking

For Eternal Life.

Ah! What a paradox.
Eternal Life is Love.

And Love knows no time,
And Love knows no space.

I want to live in that timeless,
Spaceless, eternal gaze

Of my lover, my child,
My memories

Of my first
Stage performance,

And the eternal applause
Deafening my heart.

Notes

Notes

Notes

Notes

Notes

Notes

Notes

Notes